MEET TH

# Buffy
the Vampire Slayer

# MEET THE STARS OF

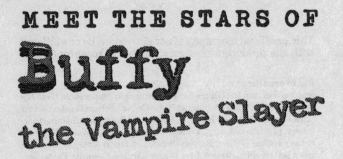

# Buffy
## the Vampire Slayer

An
UNAUTHORIZED
Biography

by Jan Gabriel

**SCHOLASTIC INC.**

New York  Toronto  London  Auckland  Sydney
Mexico City  New Delhi  Hong Kong

**Photo credits:**
**front cover:** top left (Barry King/Shooting Star); top middle (Tom Rodriguez/Globe Photos); top right (Pacha/Corbis); bottom (Pacha/Corbis)
**back cover:** left (Lesley Bohm); right (Howard Rosenberg/Shooting Star)
**insert:** p. 1 (Photofest); p. 2 (Pacha/Corbis); p. 3 top (Walter McBride/Retna); bottom (Fitzroy Barrett/Globe); p. 4 top (courtesy of *16* magazine); bottom (Photofest); p. 5 top (Roger Karnbad/Celebrity Photo); bottom (Warner Brothers/Shooting Star); p. 6 (Janet Gough/Celebrity Photo); p. 7 top (Everett Collection); bottom (Miranda Shen/Celebrity Photo); p. 8 (Barry King/Shooting Star); p. 9 top (Globe Photos); bottom (Judie Burstein/Globe Photos); p. 10 (Miranda Shen/Celebrity Photo); p. 11 top (Globe Photos); bottom (Globe Photos); p. 12 (Christopher Voelker/Shooting Star); p. 13 top (Steve Granitz/Retna); bottom (Globe Photos); p. 14 (Lesley Bohm); p. 15 top (Everett Collection); bottom (Everett Collection); p. 16 (Globe Photos)

ISBN 0-590-51477-6

Cover and insert designed by Joan Ferrigno

12 11 10 9 8 7 6 5 4 3 2 1          8 9/9 0 1 2 3/0
Printed in the U.S.A.
First Scholastic printing, December 1998

# Contents

**Introduction**                                          1

**Chapter 1:** Sarah Michelle Gellar:
Before She Was the Slayer                                 5

**Chapter 2:** Sarah's Teen Trauma-rama                   15

**Chapter 3:** New Girl in Town:
Sarah Arrives on
*All My Children*                                         26

**Chapter 4:** She *Is* the Slayer —
The Buffy Story                                           38

**Chapter 5:** Living in the Now                          50

**Chapter 6:** I Know What You Did . . .
and How You *Scream*ed!                                   61

**Chapter 7:** Nicholas Brendon as
Xander Harris                                             73

**Chapter 8:** Alyson Hannigan as
Willow Rosenberg                                          89

**Chapter 9:** David Boreanaz as Angel — 99

**Chapter 10:** Charisma Carpenter as Cordelia Chase — 113

**Chapter 11:** Seth Green as Oz — 126

**Chapter 12:** Camp *Buffy*: A Day Behind the Scenes — 136

**Chapter 13:** Quick Bites on the Slayer Team — 146

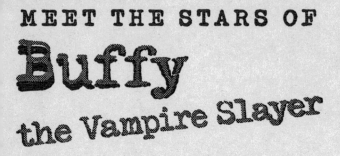

# MEET THE STARS OF
# Buffy
## the Vampire Slayer

# Introduction

## Deal With This Show for a Moment

"*In every generation there is a chosen one. She alone will stand against the vampires, the demons, and the forces of darkness. She is the slayer!*"

So begins the TV show *Buffy the Vampire Slayer* each week.

In every TV season, one show grips the imaginations of an entire generation of young viewers. In recent seasons, one show stood alone — it made stars out of its cast and put an entire network on the map!

That would be *Buffy the Vampire Slayer*.

Since its debut in March 1997, *Buffy* has vaulted from being the cellar dweller of the TV ratings chart to the most popular show among 'tweens and teens. It became so successful that it was moved from its Monday nine P.M. time slot and used to kick off an entire new night of programming, since it was felt that fans, loyal and devoted, would follow it anywhere. And they have. Tuesday nights are now *Buffy* nights — must-see TV for millions of slayer buffs.

It is now the season of the Buffster. The show is regularly praised by the critics. "The most consistently entertaining hour on TV," declared *USA Today*. "Brightest new show of the season," asserted *People* magazine. "Smart, knowing, sly, funny, sweet and respecting of teens," stated the *New York Post*. In every chronicle of pop culture, you find *Buffy* on the "It" list, the "Hit" list, the "Love at First Bite" list.

Critics cheering is good; fans knowing the real deal is better. What *is* Buffy's deal? As they say, she alone stands against the vampires and forces of darkness. But she is a teen, and she alone also has to ace those pop quizzes, be real with her buds, deal with her mom, and, *hello*, is having a social life too much to ask? Most times, yes. The horror, the horror, indeed.

Buffy Summers never asked to be the chosen one but, oops, there it is. She can't get away from being the slayer. So her choice, drummed into her by Giles, the watcher, is basically nil. A slayer's gotta do what a slayer's gotta do.

But while she's stabbing vampires, she's also taking a stab at normal life. At having friends, like Willow and Xander and Cordelia. At romance, love — maybe another chance at romance with Angel. At the constant battle to fit in, against all odds.

And against all odds, she and the show that bears her name are doing it.

Here's the how, what, why, where, and who of it all.

3

# 1

# Sarah Michelle Gellar: Before She Was the Slayer

**B**uffy Summers is the chosen one, born to vanquish vampires and dispose of other nasty forces of evil. Armed with *real* grrl power, a bag of spikes, crucifixes, and medieval power tools, plus a wise watcher and a cool posse, Buffy's entire life is "must slay." There's one in every generation and, like it or not — tag: She's It.

Sarah Michelle Gellar was the one chosen for the part of Buffy Summers. But make no mistake, in every aspect of her life, this one included, Sarah did the choosing. Blessed with burning desire, megatalent, and the support of her family, *her* entire life is "must act." Always has been.

To hear Sarah flippantly tell it, her career practically fell into her lap. "I started when I was four years old," she's said in various interviews. "Somebody came up to me in a restaurant and asked if I'd ever thought about acting. I said, 'Oh yeah, I want to do it.'"

And the rest is herstory? Not quite. It never happens exactly like that. While Sarah may have snared her first acting role fairly easily, a whole lot of hard work, rejection, sweat, and even tears sometimes went into building her career. The Sarah Michelle Gellar who plays the slayer is no overnight success story. Hardly a day of her life has gone by when she wasn't working, or trying to. Acting is what she lives for.

Sarah was born on April 14, 1977, in New York City. The only child of Steven Gellar and former schoolteacher Rosellen Gellar, Sarah was a self-described ham who commanded the spotlight and blossomed under it. "Acting was in my blood from the time I was little," she once told *Soap Opera Magazine*. "I was this big ham, and I had to do something! So I would perform for anyone who would listen or watch. I would put on little plays, or act out movies. I was very precocious, like a twenty-five-year-old trapped in a four-year-old body."

She was also absolutely adorable, with big green eyes, a button nose, a megawatt smile, and always a ready quip. It was that bright, gregarious, and adorable little girl a casting agent spied in a New York City restaurant that day. Sarah's mom was open to the suggestion that her only child give acting a shot, and followed up on it.

Sarah was cast in her first role soon after, a TV movie called *Invasion of Privacy*, starring Valerie Harper. Sarah played the daughter of Valerie's character. At first, she found it weird to call someone else "Mommy," but Sarah adapted to that more easily than to her surroundings. "We did the filming on an island in the winter, and it was freezing! I was really little — I mean I was four, but also small for my age — and there was so much snow, they hired this guy to carry me on the set because they were afraid I'd get lost in a snowdrift."

But, as happens with most teleflicks, this one aired once and was instantly forgotten. But not to Sarah. Her memories are still fresh. "I was supposed to audition with Valerie Harper," she told *Soap Opera Digest*,

7

"but she'd already gone home. So I just said, 'No problem.' First I did my lines, and then, in Valerie's voice, I did hers. I was hired on the spot."

Sarah's second big showbiz break was even more memorable — it made headlines. The job was for a commercial, and in 1982 it was the first to actually diss a competitor's product. In the Burger King ad, which aired nationally, Sarah was the tiny tike who chided McDonald's for their "stingy patties."

Oops. As Sarah recounted for a journalist, "McDonald's turned around and sued not only Burger King and the ad agency — they also sued me! I was five. I couldn't even say the *word* 'lawyer,' and a few months later, I was telling my friends, 'I can't play. I've got to give a deposition.'" Sarah can laugh about it now, because eventually the case was settled. Plus, she came out of the whole experience as the bona fide Burger King spokeskid: She did thirty more commercials for that chain.

Another showbiz reality check came soon after. Sarah needed to join the Screen Actors Guild, the union all actors are listed with. The rule is that no two actors can go by the exact same name professionally. At the time four-year-old Sarah joined, there was already a Sarah Gellar on the roster. That's the reason she had to add her middle name, Michelle, for acting jobs.

Sarah swiftly piled up the credits. Among her favorites was a guest-starring part in *Spencer: For Hire,* a hit detective series that starred Robert Urich. Sarah bonded instantly with Bob. A parent himself, Bob was sensitive and understood the unique pressures child actors are under: being away from home, friends, and school — stuff adult actors don't have to deal with. "I was eight or nine years old, and he was just wonderful to me," Sarah has said.

Other costars in her young life included Matthew Broderick and Eric Stoltz. At different times, the actors were the headliners in *The Widow Claire,* a play that ran on New York's famous Broadway; Sarah was featured for much of its run. Back then, Matthew was *the* hot teen star of the movie *Ferris Bueller's Day Off.* And Eric was no slouch in the screen dream department with his movie *Some Kind of Wonderful.*

Because of her proximity to them, Sarah's own stock went up among certain of her schoolmates. "I was the most popular girl in school because I was working with both of them," she jokingly told *Parade* magazine.

She really meant that as a joke — because more than once, she's admitted that she was far, *far* from popular back in elementary school. She attended the exclusive private school Columbia Preparatory. "Kids were hard on me. I was always excluded from everything because I was different. That's difficult when you're a child."

What made her different? Her career, mainly. "After school and on the weekends, I had to choose between going out with all the kids, or going on auditions." The latter won out nearly every single time. And it cost her. "The second you start missing school and social events, you stop getting invited to parties, and people stop talking to you," she has explained. Which *would* make it hard to have friends.

Worse than going on auditions, perhaps, were the long leaves of absence she'd often take to go off and make a movie or a TV show. "One year," Sarah recalled for the *Patriot Ledger,* "I had more absences in the first month of school than you're supposed to have for the entire year."

But apart from geographical and career-centered reasons for being virtually friendless in elementary school, Sarah has felt there were other reasons, too. "I didn't have anything in common with the kids," she told a reporter. "Many of those students were used to having everything handed to them on a silver platter. Everything I got, I worked hard for, and got on my own."

At the end of the day, Sarah totally feels the sacrifices she made back then paid off. So she wasn't among the "in" crowd at school. Instead, she ended up meeting other young actors through the rounds of auditions, callbacks, commercials, and other showbiz-related events. She found her peer group among kids who were making similar choices and dealing with the same stuff. Included in those friends: Jenna Von Oy, who went on to costar in *Blossom,* and Melissa Joan Hart, aka *Sabrina the Teenage Witch.*

Sarah's memories of hanging with Melissa are still strong. They'd run into each other at auditions, where they often competed for the same role. But any rivalry ended the minute they walked out the casting director's door. "After auditions, we'd all go out to eat, me and my mom, Melissa and her mom, and all her brothers and sisters," Sarah has said. Although she has admitted to occasional twinges of envy for Melissa's large, loving clan of six siblings, Sarah wasn't family-deprived.

Sarah's best friend in those years was probably her mom, Rosellen Gellar. Although Rosellen worked as a nursery school teacher, she was always there for her daughter physically and emotionally, as chauffeur, cook, and confidante — everything *but* stage mother. Sarah used to bristle at the mere suggestion. "My mom is not living vicariously through me," Sarah once told a journalist who dared to suggest it. "It has always been my choice to act. If at any time I wanted to give it up, she would be behind me one hundred percent."

Sarah's dad hasn't been in the picture for a long time. Steven and Rosellen broke up when Sarah was seven. In interviews about that, Sarah would invariably answer with a terse, "I don't see my real dad. We never got along and he's out of the picture." She'd usually follow up with a sunny response about her stepdad. "He's the one who sat in the front row at school recitals with the camera," she'd say.

Rosellen Gellar tried hard to see that Sarah had a normal childhood, despite her daughter's busy career, by enrolling her in extracurricular "regular kid stuff."

Sarah Michelle Gellar, regular kid? Not really. She couldn't help excelling at everything she did. She didn't just take ice-skating lessons. "I placed third in the New York State regional figure skating competition the only year I competed," Sarah has proudly recalled.

She started lessons in the martial art of tae kwon do at age eight. "All the girls took ballet, but I wanted to do something different," Sarah has noted of her choice. She stuck with it for eleven years — and, yep, she rocked, describing, "I placed fourth in the Madison Square Garden Karate Championships."

Perhaps one of the reasons she did quit was because her mom felt Sarah was trying to pack too much into her young life — and something had to give. "I was going to school, acting, skating, and doing tae kwon do all at one time," Sarah once explained. "And my mom's rule was, if my grades slip below A mi-

13

nus, I had to stop working. So she sat me down one day and said, 'You can pick two things; you can't do them all. And school has to be one of them.' So I choose acting as the other."

The choice surprised no one. Even when she wasn't working, she spent a lot of time watching and learning from the work of others. The TV was on constantly at her house. She even admits to taping daytime soaps when she was at school. "They're fun," she explained when asked. "It's like an escape." In fact, when she had a choice between watching kid shows like *Saved by the Bell* or adult soaps like *Knots Landing*, she always went with the grown-up choice.

But being *in* a children's show — or any show — was exactly what she wanted.

# 2

# Sarah's Teen Trauma-rama

While Sarah's acting career was off to a smooth start, life in the reality zone was bumpier than ever. Her worst time, perhaps, was junior high school. Admittedly a tough period for most 'tweens and teens, junior high was its own little horror show for the girl who'd one day be the slayer. More than once, Sarah's declared, "Junior high school was my *Buffy* experience."

It was, she insists, a painful time. At the age of twelve, she enrolled in LaGuardia Junior High School, a private school. But not, Sarah stresses, for any elitist reason. "Even though it seems odd to people in the Midwest, everyone goes to private school in Manhattan." While that's not entirely accurate, it probably is true for a large percentage of the upper-middle-class and wealthy kids in Sarah's neighborhood.

Sarah was miserable at that school. She didn't fit in, but not because her classmates all had more money than she did. "I was not popular to the extreme. I was the girl nobody liked, who was weird and quirky. I felt different and awkward. And it didn't help that I was a nerd," she told the on-line *Mr. Showbiz*. "I was very into my studies."

Sarah claims she did make some stabs at fitting in but, perhaps because they were halfhearted, they didn't work out. "I tried to be a jock. I tried to be cool. But I couldn't find my place."

Missing a lot of school did little to up her rep. Once again, she had to make work-vs.-social-life choices. "I always had to choose between stuff like a slumber party, a school dance — and another audition." As usual, she mostly chose the latter. "I was always missing classes and extracurricular activities. I missed the eighth-grade trip to Busch Gardens because I was filming a TV movie."

It didn't help that Sarah was, at heart, kind of shy. "In a roomful of people I don't

16

know, like at a party, I'll just sit in a corner with one or two people. I'm always uncomfortable around people my own age. I'm much more comfortable when I'm at work." Fortunately for her, work was plentiful. For all through those years, Sarah continued racking up credits on her résumé. In 1991, she was picked for her highest-profile role to date, in the TV movie *A Woman Named Jackie,* a biopic of Jacqueline Kennedy Onassis. Three young actresses portrayed Young Jackie at different ages; Sarah had the role of our former First Lady as a teenager. She was only in a few scenes, but careerwise, Sarah considers it a big break.

Painting a totally bleak picture of Sarah's own young teen years wouldn't be fair. For outside of school — apart from acting, even — Sarah was doing much better. "I'm a typical teenager. When I'm bored, I want to change my hair color," she half joked to *People* magazine when she was fifteen.

She did, after all, have girlfriends to hang with, even though they were other actresses, some of whom were a good deal older than her. Eva LaRue, who worked with Sarah on the TV soap *All My Children,* was for a time

Sarah's closest bud, despite a ten-year age gap. Shopping, talking on the phone, and dancing were her favorite things to do with friends.

She also found time for family vacations. In 1992, her mom remarried, and the little family of three did some traveling. Sarah's favorite destination in those days was the beach. "Bermuda is my favorite place to relax, and Aruba is the best place to party."

Sarah's life changed for the better in high school when she switched schools halfway through, moving to New York City's Professional Children's School. Among its alumni are Christina Ricci and Macaulay Culkin.

"It's an amazing place," Sarah enthused in an on-line interview. "It's for anyone with irregular schedules — kids who are musicians from the Juilliard School of Music, ballerinas from the School of American Ballet, and writers. Just the most talented group of young people. It's a place where your talent is special, but it doesn't affect your schoolwork. Everybody here has a talent, and everyone is respected. If somebody doesn't like you, they simply don't talk to you. They don't make fun of you or punish you. You can mess around with how you dress. You really have that chance to find yourself, and I thank God for that school. It was my lifeline."

Some of her high-school memories are academic. *Earth in the Balance*, by Vice President Al Gore, was a book on her required reading list that influenced her greatly. "When I got the assignment," she once admitted to a reporter, "I wasn't thrilled about it. But the book turned out to be so brilliant. As I read it, I can't believe how true everything he's saying is. It's about how humans are destroying nature, and there is this whole chapter on spirituality. I think this book should be read by the whole country."

Clearly, she felt much more comfortable at Professional Children's School, yet she remained outside the mainstream. "Even there, I was more Willow than Buffy," she insists. Mostly it was because, as usual, she wasn't there a lot. Her dilemma over tough choices remained the same. "I had to decide between going to my junior prom and going to the Emmys," she mentioned to a reporter. "I went to the Emmys, but at least I got to go to the after-prom party."

All told, Sarah only spent two and a half years in high school, not because she dropped out. She simply — well, but not so simply —

worked double time and completed two years in one. "Most actors just go home after work and learn their lines for the next day. I'd go home, do geometry, algebra, and all my other subjects — then memorize the script and learn my lines."

She did it all, and did it all amazingly well. By 1994, she'd earned her diploma.

No matter how well she met the challenges that came her way, Sarah got sick of hearing the same question over again: "Don't you feel you gave up your childhood?" But ever the pro, she aimed for gracious answers — mostly. "I was not meant to be in Little League or the local ballet school," she said on one occasion. "I'm tired of people who say acting corrupts young people. You know what? There are a lot of actors who've been working since a young age, and they're just fine."

Another perk of her chosen childhood lifestyle was jetting off to exotic locations and experiencing things most kids never do. "I traveled all over the world while I was growing up," she said, adding that while it was often for work or for vacation, her mom made sure she learned something. "Part of the rules my mom set were that whenever we were in a city for six days, the seventh day we'd do something educational so I could learn about the city. We'd go to museums and other places of local interest."

Working with adults taught her other lessons. In an interview, she said, "I learned how to talk to people, how to be social, things that a lot of kids don't know. I've found that kids in high school are often clones of each other, but this — being an actress — gave me an individual personality. A lot of kids go through college and try to find themselves, but I know who I am."

## *Swan's Crossing*: The First 'Tween Soap

Before 1992, Sarah had done commercials, guest-star gigs on TV, and the occasional movie or teleflick. In 1992, she nailed her first regular TV role.

The show was called *Swan's Crossing,* and it ran for sixty-five episodes. But if you don't remember it, there's a good reason. Syndicated, it aired on different channels across the country at random times during the day — or night. *Swan's Crossing* had the bad luck to be on at the weirdest times — like six A.M. Still, the show had a great concept, and in an important way it boosted Sarah's career.

21

*Swan's Crossing* was conceived as the first TV soap opera aimed at 'tweens and teens. All its major characters were teens. They all lived in and around a posh East Coast seaside town, Swan's Crossing. The story lines were "predictable" soap standards, pitting the privileged rich kids against the tougher other-side-of-the-tracks kids, creating *Romeo-and-Juliet*-inspired romances among the kids of feuding families, and, of course, bringing strangers with mysterious backgrounds into town.

"We will explore the stormy relationships and exciting adventures of the kids, who are rich enough to act out their fantasies and interesting enough to keep multiple intrigues and stories going," detailed the show's producer. Or, as fifteen-year-old Sarah Michelle Gellar explained in *Entertainment Weekly,* "We do things like, 'your best friend is mean,' or 'you have a guy your parents don't like,' stuff we can all relate to. It's good to know that what's going on with you is happening to everyone else — and you're not alone out there."

In another interview she boasted that *Swan's Crossing* was going to give another teen-themed TV'er — *90210* — a run for its money. Although Sarah was often chosen as spokesperson, she was far from alone on the show: There were a whopping twelve young regulars in the cast.

Sarah played the central role of Sydney Rutledge, the spoiled young heiress to one of the town's most established, old-moneyed families. A champion equestrian, Sydney was the self-designated social leader of her set. Rich and pampered, she drove herself to be first at everything — no matter what the cost or who got hurt along the way.

Bluntly put, she wasn't a real sympathetic character.

And behind the scenes, in the opinion of one reporter, anyway, Sarah wasn't very different. During one group interview, she politely declined to be included. She wouldn't pose for individual pictures as the others did; instead, she handed out her glamour publicity head shot. And although she finally agreed to pose with her cast mates for a couple of group pictures, she wouldn't wear a magazine-logo baseball cap like the others did.

No question, Sarah was by far the most experienced of her peers, most of whom were unknown then, as now. Aside from Sarah, two of them have gone on to greater fame.

Shane McDermott played rich rebel Garrett Booth in *Swan's Crossing*. He went on to star in a series of widely aired public service announcements, the movie *Airborne,* and other afternoon TV shows.

Brittany Daniel, who played Mila Rosnovsky, chief rival to Sarah's character, went on to TV acclaim with her twin sister, Cynthia, as the star of TV's teen based-on-the-book-series saga *Sweet Valley High.*

Irked reporters aside, Sarah seemed to get along with her costars. *Swan's Crossing* was filmed in the New York City borough of Queens, at Kaufman-Astoria Studios (made famous as *The Cosby Show*'s locale). Dressing rooms were shared, two to a room, and a schoolroom was set up backstage where tutors gathered to make sure no one missed a lesson. Most of the young actors were friends off the set as well.

In spite of all it had going for it, the show never went on to a second season. *Swan's Crossing* may have bombed, but it would lead to better and much bigger things for Sarah.

*Entertainment Weekly* unwittingly predicted it when they described Sarah's *Swan's* character as a "young Erica Kane." The magazine was referring to the character played by Susan Lucci on *All My Children*. And that, in fact, would be Sarah's next gig. The character she created was the daughter of Erica Kane, one Kendall Hart. It would make Sarah a star.

extra was referring to the operator played by Susan Lucci on *All My Children*. And that in fact would be Gellar's next role. The character she created was the daughter of Erica Kane, one, Kendall Hart. Or would make such a mark.

## 3

# New Girl in Town: Sarah Arrives on *All My Children*

ABC-TV's *All My Children* premiered seven years before Sarah Michelle Gellar was born. An afternoon soap opera, it takes place in fictional Pine Valley, USA.

One of the key characters on *All My Children* is the resident heartbreaker/home-wrecker Erica Kane, the classic vixen found in all soaps. In 1993, the writers decided to give her a jolt: the return of a daughter she'd given up for adoption at the baby's birth. The girl, who'd arrive in Pine Valley unannounced, would be one angry, revenge-seeking, havoc-wreaking babe. The target of her long-boiling wrath? The mother who abandoned her — Erica Kane. And in most ways, the daughter would prove to be every bit as deliciously deceptive as the woman who spawned her.

She'd be called Kendall Hart.

Casting Kendall was a megachallenge, because the young actress would have to hold her own against Susan Lucci, who'd arguably created the most famous daytime TV character ever. By 1993, the name Erica Kane was synonymous with vixen. Whoever snagged the Kendall role had to be an actress of great range and ability — she had, after all, to match wits with her TV mom and win a few battles as well. The tall order was filled by a small-of-stature yet powerful young actress: Sarah Michelle Gellar.

*She had absolutely no idea what she was getting into.*

As Sarah told a magazine back then, "I didn't know when I auditioned for Kendall that she would turn out to be [so nasty]. I had heard rumors, but they were squelched very quickly." She also wasn't told right off the secret of Kendall's true identity.

What she did know made her want the role. For one thing, as a viewer Sarah had been a huge fan of TV soaps. As a working actress, she knew this: "[Soaps] are an amazing training ground. There's nothing like them; unlike theater, there's a new script every day. The amount of work you do on a soap cannot be compared to anything else — how little time you have to prepare for the huge amount of actual work."

And she also knew that playing Kendall was a huge opportunity. "In this business," she told a reporter, "if you're a teenager, it's hard to get a role that has any meat to it. So to get Kendall was amazing. I feel lucky because it's so rare. They just don't write for kids; you usually have older people playing younger." And that was the coolest part of all: Sarah, who auditioned when she was fifteen, would break the mold by playing *older.*

None of that helped her major case of the jitters her first day on the set. By that time she knew she'd be working alongside the legendary Susan Lucci — and finally learned that Kendall was her long-lost daughter. Sarah described her reaction, gulping, "I'm . . . her what? Daughter? Me?"

Sarah's stint on *All My Children* began in March 1993. "I was very nervous," she has admitted. "I kept thinking, 'What if I'm really bad and they fire me?'" As it turned out, she needn't have worried. "On my first day, I walked in and snuck in the back behind the coffee machine to watch Susan and Michael Nader rehearse a scene. All of a sudden Susan said, 'Hold it, we need to stop for a minute,' and she walked over to me and said, 'Congratulations! I'm very glad you're here.' Then she introduced me to everyone. She really helped me and always made sure I was okay during my first couple of weeks."

Helping, too, was the smiling face of Lindsay Price, her friend from Professional Children's School who was also on the show.

It didn't take long for Sarah to slip comfortably into Kendall's shoes. Correction: She understood her character well; she didn't necessarily relate to her. Kendall, of course, was a lying manipulator, deviously determined to use anyone to achieve her goal of making Erica's life miserable. Sarah was fully convincing in the role. So convincing that, after several months, she found herself having to assure the press — and the public — that in real life she was nothing like her backbiting character. "The only trait we have in common is determination," she told a soap magazine, adding, "There are no other qualities she has that I want!"

If Sarah felt comfortable playing Kendall, the public's reaction to her in the role was just as positive. She was an instant smash, even credited with revitalizing the show. *People* magazine gushed, "She brought life back into the twenty-four-year-old soap."

In the beginning, especially, *All My Children* was a happy time for Sarah. For a girl who loved to work as much as she did, the show provided it aplenty. Plus, Kendall soon became a lightning rod; many plots revolved around her. During her first fourteen months in Pine Valley, Kendall tried to break up her mother and stepfather, purposely left her eight-year-old sister alone with a bad guy, and did other spiteful deeds.

Sarah ate it up. "It's amazing playing a psycho loony! She is definitely the most terrible daughter in daytime," Sarah reported gleefully. "I don't always agree with her methods, but as an actress, I have to justify her actions — and I do. It's a great way to get out my frustrations!"

*All My Children*'s New York City set became the social center of her world as well. For that's where she cemented her friendship with Lindsay Price — who became the closest thing to a best friend Sarah had ever had. "We learn our lines together," Sarah told a reporter. "We keep each other company, do homework together if we have time." Mostly, the girls ordered lots of Chinese food to be delivered to their shared dressing room. "I've got to have it at least three times a week," Sarah told a reporter. "We're very lucky that they clean out our dressing rooms every day, because Lindsay and I have a problem with that! There's Chinese food everywhere!"

Although things would change later on, at first she even got on well with her TV mom, Susan Lucci. Sarah was in awe of the actress's talent. "I watch Susan and I marvel at how she does it," the nervous novice admitted to a reporter early on. "I'm always worried about where I'm going to stand and what I'm going to say. She does it effortlessly."

In fact, Sarah's *AMC* attitude was summed up in this quote: "I can't believe they're paying me to do this!"

No one can pinpoint exactly when things started to change, least of all Sarah. But after a while, other quotes began to surface in the press — more complaints than compliments. At first, Sarah's objections centered on her workload. "It was very, very difficult," Sarah said once. "I was the only contract player [daily costar] under the age of eighteen — because of the hectic schedule, few soaps even have younger people on them. I was surrounded by adults, with an intense amount of work, learning forty pages of dialogue a day; shooting an episode a day; still trying to graduate high school at the same time. After working all day, it took me an hour just to unwind."

And then there were the tabloids. Along with praise for her acting came scrutiny from the celebrity-soaked press: Sarah found herself teen tab bait. As the July 1, 1995, issue of *TV Guide* conceded, "The supermarket tabs have had a field day with this actress practically since her arrival at *AMC*." What dirt could they possibly have had back then on sixteen-year-old Sarah? Well, none, actually; so they created some. According to the *TV Guide* article, one rag photographed Sarah, her costar Sydney Penny, and Sydney's fiancé, Rob Powers, arriving at an ABC Christmas party. Then they cropped Sydney out of the shot, making it appear as if Sarah were stealing her friend's intended.

Of course, the tabloids really went to town when reports of bad blood between Sarah and Susan Lucci started to surface. If the magazines had been looking for something bad to say about Sarah before, this time they didn't have to look too far. For this time, there *was* a shred of truth to the rumors. And the tabs played it — overplayed it, really — for more than it was worth.

Some reports said Susan, the pro, was jealous. They painted Ms. Lucci as a vengeful, insecure diva who couldn't bear acting opposite a younger, prettier, more talented version of herself.

Others said it was sneaky Sarah causing the dustups. They characterized her as a pint-sized prima donna who took delight in pushing Susan's emotional buttons.

So what *was* the deal between teenage Sarah Michelle Gellar and top-of-her-field icon Susan Lucci? Even today, years later, both actresses have too much class to publicly air what went on between them — but by now, no one's denying that major issues did crop up.

At first, however, both were publicly diplomatic, pooh-poohing rumors of discord. As time went on, Sarah became terse when quizzed about the relationship. "Susan's a pro," was the sum total of her respectful response. It wasn't until she'd left the show that Sarah felt free enough to be more honest. "We didn't have the best working relationship," she admitted to the press. "I denied it for a long time, because that's what you're supposed to do. But," she insisted, "it was never as bad as people made it out to be. We didn't hang out off the set; we weren't going to lunch. We worked together, on top of each other — the problems were inevitable." Eventually, Sarah admitted, "It wasn't an easy time in my life."

The Daytime Emmy Awards made it less easy. Many people know Susan Lucci as the actress with many Emmy nominations (eighteen to date) but no Emmy win. In 1994, she was nominated in her usual "Outstanding Lead Actress" category. That was the same year Sarah Michelle Gellar was nominated for the first time ever. Her category was "Outstanding Younger Actress." Sarah was pumped. "I can't even put into words how excited I was to be nominated," she gushed back then.

She didn't win, but some have said the nomination itself increased the on-set tension. The next year, the same two were nominated; and this time, Sarah did win. It was a major big deal.

"It's amazing," she told an audience of TV critics. "It's one of those things that everybody dreams about. You do your work and it's wonderful that people respect it. That's what the Emmy was to me, proof that people respected and enjoyed my work."

But by 1995, nearly three seasons after joining *All My Children,* Sarah no longer enjoyed her work. Forget the Susan Lucci deal; there were big-time other reasons for the season of Sarah's discontent. For one thing, Kendall's story lines had dwindled to one day a week: The creative fulfillment Sarah always craved was suddenly not being met.

Worse, her contract prevented her from taking other roles. "I was offered two other projects, which [the bosses at *AMC*] did not release me to do. And to be honest, I was a little bitter about that." Anyone would have been, since the roles were for major motion pictures: *The Crucible* and . . . the big ouch, *William Shakespeare's Romeo + Juliet*.

So how much was Sarah *not* enjoying *All My Children*? Quietly, behind the scenes and six months prior to the Emmys, she'd informed the producers that she was quitting. But in the "bad timing of epic proportions award," the news of Sarah's "buh-bye" to the show broke just as she accepted her Emmy. Oops.

To some, it looked like she was ungrateful. To others, it looked like she was fired at the command of a vengeful also-ran Susan Lucci. And to still more, it looked like Sarah quit because she suddenly got too big for her daytime britches. It looked . . . bad.

Sarah tried valiantly to spin-control the situation. "The timing didn't make me look good, like, oh look, she won an Emmy, now she's gone. But I had made the decision to leave six months earlier." And, "I was not competing against Susan," she reminded the press. "She's in the leading actress category, I was in the younger actress category. And let's be honest — hers is a much more difficult category. And I won for the scenes I submitted with her. You don't work alone. This was work we did together."

The collective response to her attempt at diplomacy? What*ever*. The outcome remained the same. Sarah, clutching her Emmy, sailed away.

# 4

# She *Is* the Slayer —
# The Buffy Story

### *"This Is What I've Waited for
My Whole Life!"*

Buffy's got buzz. Now, that is. It didn't always. Actually, the fact that *Buffy the Vampire Slayer* became the signature show of a brand-new network and is among the fastest-growing shows on TV qualifies as one large chunk of "who'da thunk it?" Because its beginnings were beyond humble.

*Buffy the Vampire Slayer* started out in 1990 as a germ of an idea. Its creator, screenwriter Joss Whedon, told *Time* magazine how the idea came to him. He'd spent years watching horror movies in which "bubble-headed blonds" (his expression) wandered into dark alleys and got attacked by some creature. He explained, "I'd love to see a movie in which the blond wanders into a dark alley, takes care of herself, and deploys her powers." Furthermore, Joss thought that the blond should be in high school — her terrifying encounters with those creatures of the night would mirror all the anxieties kids really experience there.

Although Joss is genetically predisposed to be a Hollywood screenwriter — his grandfather and father wrote episodes of *Mayberry, RFD; Alice;* and *Benson* — *he* was still little known in 1992. But that's when he got the chance to make his movie. It was called *Buffy the Vampire Slayer.*

It bombed big-time. Instead of rocking the big screen with kickin' girl power, *Buffy* the movie wimped out. It starred starlet Kristy Swanson as the Buffster, and it was played for comic camp. Trivia alert: Aside from its quirky title, the main reason it attracted any attention at all was for costar Luke Perry. At the time, the *90210* hipster was white-hot, and this was the project he picked to make his movie debut. What he liked about it, Luke had said rather presciently, was precisely that he wasn't the star. So the movie tanks, it wasn't his failure, no one could point the finger at him.

Smooth move, dude. No one did blame him when *Buffy* went down. The movie was soon forgotten. But not by everyone.

How it got resurrected into a TV show is pure Hollywood. In the years between big and little screen *Buffy*s, Joss Whedon cowrote the screenplay for another movie. This one, *Toy Story*, became a huge box office smash and put him on the map. His writing contributions to *Speed* and *Twister* solidified his rep. This freshly minted clout suddenly put Joss in the Hollywood driver's seat. So where'd he want to go? Back to Sunnydale, the Hellmouth of the world.

Why go back to *Buffy* land? To fix it. For the movie he'd envisioned was not the movie that came out: He'd never intended it to be a comedy, but a dark, scary horror picture with comic elements — a teenage *X-Files* with a dash of *Clueless* thrown in. A show that, as Buffy might say, would give fans "the wiggins." If Joss could make the movie into a TV series, he could get it right.

Why'd the WB network want it? "There were no TV shows out there pitched to young girls," explained an executive. They were looking for a show that girls could relate to. "Buffy faces all the things you go through in high school — from a date that goes wrong to a final exam that seems impossible. But she also has to keep the world safe from vampires."

In early 1996, a deal was struck. A script for the pilot episode was written — and the search for the ideal Buffster was launched.

Joss's vision for the TV Buffy was drastically different from the dopey valley girl of the movie. He wanted a Buffy who was possessed — of killer looks, slayer smarts, fully empowered, if a bit school challenged. He wanted her to be conflicted: Should she go to the prom or pummel a vampire? He wanted her to have more depth, more angst than the movie eye-candy heroine. He wanted a lonely girl isolated by her slayer status. Upshot: He wanted a teen slayer for the millennium.

Where to find such a tough Buff?

*He* certainly didn't know that his Buffy was three thousand miles away. But *she* did.

Flashback to 1993. Sarah Michelle Gellar is playing Kendall on *All My Children*. The *Buffy* video comes out, and *AMC*'s makeup artist, Norman, notes a striking resemblance

41

between Sarah and Kristy Swanson. Sarah finds it so amusing that she begins a three-year-long running joke, quoting lines from the movie to him in her best Buffy-speak.

And then, in 1996, she hears, via the showbiz grapevine, about plans for a *Buffy* TV show. Destiny called!

Only, *Buffy*'s producers thought . . . not.

With visions of the evil Kendall in their collective minds — not to mention that über-cool Emmy she'd won — she was asked to audition for the role of snobby, manipulative Cordelia. Sarah did read for that part, then turned around and begged to be considered for the lead.

Much auditioning ensued. "I probably had eleven auditions and four screen tests," she said in an interview. "It was the most awful experience of my life, but I was so driven. I thought, 'I'm going to have this role.'"

Joss confirms Sarah's story — with his tongue firmly in cheek. "We cast her first as Cordelia," he conceded to *Seventeen* magazine. "She insists she auditioned nineteen times for Buffy — but that's a total exaggeration. It wasn't more than seventeen times!"

Aside from her powerful feeling that she was destined for this role, there *were* other reasons Sarah went after the part so vigorously. She loved the girl-power premise and found it way relatable. "No matter how popular or unpopular you are, high school is a scary place, and we touch on that a lot. Maybe people can't always relate to the horror aspect of our show, but you can relate to the fact that high school is hard. High school is scary. What's wonderful is that all of us [Buffy, Xander, Willow, Cordelia, Oz] are going through it differently — we cover all aspects of that."

Sarah elaborated in another interview, "The themes of the show are common — loving a friend, being at an age when you're having mom problems, wanting to be an adult, and wanting to be a child at the same time. The scariest horror exists in reality. It's feeling invisible at times. Teens can understand and relate, because this is what's happening to them. What can be more horrific than high school?"

The role itself was one she could (bad comparison alert) sink her teeth into. Buffy is not some cardboard kick-butt character. "You get to play every emotion, because Buffy is an outcast," Sarah once said on-line. "She doesn't fit in. She doesn't know if she wants to be a cheerleader or fight vampires — and that's what makes her so interesting and believable. Buffy is a person who is lost, and who doesn't know where she belongs. And you feel for her."

Sarah cheered Buffy's spirit. "I always wanted to play a strong, feminine character who makes mistakes. Buffy has an amazing spirit and I hope that is never broken. She always finds something positive — even with all the evil she is surrounded by. She is not the most popular, nor the most beautiful girl at school, nor the funniest, and for sure not the smartest. She's like, 'This is who I am, and *I* like me.' What our show stresses is individuality. Buffy is a total individual, which is wonderful because she proves you don't have to fit in. You can be different and still find happiness. That's what makes Buffy a wonderful role model for lots of different types of people."

Most of all, Sarah herself related to Buffy. The character has to decide between an age-appropriate event, like the school dance or a date, and work obligations, i.e, being on patrol and slaying vampires. During Sarah's entire school career, she felt much the same. She always had to choose between a social life and her work. "[Buffy's dilemma] is something I think I understand," she said ruefully.

Once Sarah stepped into her role, she quickly got into slayer shape. She signed up for classes in kickboxing and street fighting and, most important, resumed her old tae kwon do training. "It's really an art form," she said. "I never actually used it in combat." Not that Sarah would be doing all her own stunts, but she had to look as if she could.

While Sarah was getting prepared, the rest of the casting process got underway. Since every slayer needs a watcher-slash-resident expert on all things evil, the part of school librarian Rupert Giles was key. Signing Anthony Stewart Head was a coup. Not only was he an accomplished British stage actor, but he was known to the American audience as the romantic lead in the famous Taster's Choice commercials.

Buffy also needed a posse of peers who *had* to be believable. Is anything more real in high school than unrequited crushing? So the part of Xander, the bright, funny, quasi-geek who pines for Buffy, was created, and then the part of Willow, the shy computer girl who pines for Xander. Nicholas Brendon and Alyson Hannigan won those roles and were quickly established as Buffy's confidantes and closest friends.

The slayer needed a rival, too: Enter Cordelia, a model-beautiful social climber who at first looked down her nose at the Buffy bunch. Charisma Carpenter was the choice for that role.

The part of Buffy's well-intentioned but clueless (at first, anyway) mom was given to the talented Kristine Sutherland.

There was one more character to cast. They couldn't send Buffy into the Hellmouth without a sweetie, could they? Not just any crush object would do. The babe who'd capture Buffy's heart had to be someone dangerous, someone mysterious, someone — or some*thing* — whose love for her was totally doomed. Poof! They created Angel: a vampire in love with a slayer. What could be more gut-wrenching, more deliciously dark and twisted? Tall, dark, and hunky David Boreanaz sank his fangs — oops — teeth into the role.

With the major players in place, the slaying — that is, the filming — began! In preparation for a September 1996 debut, the cast, crew, writers, producers, and directors worked nonstop. They wanted to get as many of the thirteen episodes as possible shot before the premiere. It was rigorous. It meant eighteen-hour days, seven days a week. It took most of the year to do.

After all the hurry-up part came the waiting. And waiting.

In September 1996 the fall TV season began — but the schedule was curiously *Buffy*-devoid. The show had been suddenly shelved, with little public explanation. But Sarah knew why. "It wasn't ready," she admitted later on. "The time in between [when it was supposed to go on the air and when it did] gave us a chance to fully develop and flesh out the show. It became stronger."

Which is how it happened that all thirteen episodes were filmed and "in the can" (showbiz-speak for all done, filmed and edited) and the cast had dispersed before one episode ever aired. It did finally, in March 1997, at midseason.

An instant smash? Not. Although *Buffy* was a crit hit — all the TV critics raved about it — that didn't draw audiences to the show. Ratings at first were dismal. It was blamed partly on *Buffy*'s lead-in, the touching family drama *7th Heaven,* whose audience was not necessarily up for — or old enough for — the horror-action-drama-comedy that followed. But eventually some found it, and word of mouth spread like an oil spill, fast and furiously.

It took the airing of all thirteen episodes for *Buffy*'s audience to find the show — but when they did, ardent fans made it a massive hit. Web sites and cybershrines (to all the cast members, but most heavily to Buffy and Angel) sprouted up, and the ratings began to climb. By the time *Buffy the Vampire Slayer* began season two, in September 1997, it debuted with the highest numbers ever for a WB show. During the season, ratings jumped a whopping 217 percent among teens and 'tweens from the show's start.

To mark the show's new success, a few small changes were made. While the title would formally stay *BTVS*, it would increasingly be referred to, in ads and press releases, as simply *Buffy*. That's exactly what happened when *Beverly Hills, 90210* became a hit — suddenly, it was just *90210*.

A time slot change happened in January 1998: *Buffy* was moved out of Monday nights and used to kick off the WB's "New Tuesday."

The show that followed it, *Dawson's Creek,* became a hit — totally helped by its *Buffy* lead-in.

Bottom line: *Buffy* was must-see, appointment TV. For which no one was more grateful than the Buffster herself. She was the star of a hit show that she believed in and loved. Sarah put it simply, "This is what I've waited for my whole life."

# 5

# Living in the Now

What's Sarah Michelle Gellar like when she leaves the *Buffy* set? Beyond close friends and family, not many really know — which is exactly the way Sarah wants it. Correction: It's how she designed it. Perhaps she's felt burned by her past press experience, or maybe it's just her nature, but Sarah works hard on keeping up the fence she's built between her public persona and her private life. She doesn't apologize for it. "I work very hard to maintain a separate life outside of what I do. Privacy is something I value," she told a reporter.

\*　　\*　　\*

Still, a few clues to Sarah's real deal have emerged.

**She's aggressive.** She doesn't wait for things to come to her — she goes after what she wants, especially acting roles.

**She's outgoing and friendly.** And does everything at warp speed, especially talking. When that characteristic was pointed out to her by a reporter, she explained, "I hate doing interviews, so I talk fast. The faster I finish, the better it is for me."

**Yet she's not really a reluctant superstar.** "I'm tired and I complain sometimes, but this is my career and I love it," Sarah has said. She enjoys her fame, as long as it's on her terms. To promote *Buffy,* she agreed to tons of interviews, photo shoots, and talk shows such as *Late Night With David Letterman, Regis and Kathie Lee,* and *MTV Live.* During the summer of 1998, she appeared on those warm, fuzzy ads for the WB lineup. In fact, she loves being on magazine covers, claiming, "It's one of those things you dream about." And she didn't turn down the chance at the ultimate "you've made it": a "Where's Your Milk Mustache?" ad.

**She's cool and confident.** Boasting to *Mr. Showbiz* on-line, she said, "I think I get places because of my brains and my intelligence and my talent. I never think about my looks."

**She can be sarcastic.** But she's quick to deflect criticism: "No ill will is ever intended. Sarcasm is a defense mechanism."

**She's self-deprecating.** "The scariest scene in *I Know What You Did Last Summer*," she joked, "was me in a bathing suit!"

**She can be a bit spacey.** Once she sort of left the house before dressing completely. She confessed in *Movieline*, "One day, when I'm driving to work, I have my [convertible] top down, and I'm noticing people looking at me and I'm thinking, 'I must be looking good today!' Then I look down and realize that I put my slip and my boots on, but I never put my dress on! I completely forgot to get dressed!"

**She admits to bouts of worry** — not about another dressing disconnect, but just about life in general. "I've been feeling a little intimidated by everything," she confessed to *TV Guide*. "This is what I've waited for my whole life, and now it's happening. I worry that I'm going to jinx it, that something will go wrong. There's this little voice inside me that keeps going, 'Uh-oh, things are going too well.' It makes me kind of nervous."

## Kickin' It With Friends

Sarah's off-screen haunts include her new home, high atop the Hollywood Hills. It's the first one she's owned all by herself, though her mom, Rosellen, now lives nearby in L.A. too.

You can also find Sarah at Starbucks, at fun places such as the Hard Rock Cafe, and even at theme parks such as tourist-addled Knott's Berry Farm. On one recent trip there, she suffered a *Buffy*-inspired lapse. A phony vampire jumped out and, instinctively, she gave him a karate chop. Oops. "I'd been working until five A.M.," she had to explain to the poor guy.

"I'm basically pretty normal," Sarah has said. "I like to hang out with my friends, Rollerblade, hike, go ice skating and water-skiing, go to the movies — and sometimes I even like to relax."

While the last one would be hard to prove, the others aren't. The friends she refers to include some from her New York days, Brittany and Ashley, and her California costars. She not only hangs with *Buffy* buds Alyson and Charisma, she also does the girl-bonding thing with movie costars such as Neve Campbell (*Scream 2*). Another scary movie compadre, Freddie Prinze Jr. (*I Know What You Did Last Summer*), remained on Sarah's close-friend list. Freddie, in fact, once surprised Sarah by showing up at her house fully prepared to cook her a huge dinner because he feared for her eating habits.

"I'm so lucky to have good friends, because there are days lately when I really feel like I'm in over my head," she confessed.

## A Passion for Fashion

Buffy Summers has a killer wardrobe. Stretch pants, short skirts, high boots, tank tops, and camisoles comprise her look, whether she's strolling the halls of Sunnydale High by day or patrolling vamp-infested graveyards by night. Natch, she never leaves home without her most necessary accessories: crucifix, stake, and tool kit.

The Buffy look comes courtesy of the WB network's cutting edge costume designer, Cynthia Bergstrom, who told *In Style* magazine, "[Buffy's] clothes are very fashionable, but also affordable."

Affordable? You make the call — for Buffy is such the designer-clad slayer. Her T-shirts are CK and Parallel; her skirts come from BCBG; those cute little sweaters are Dolce &

Gabbana; that powder blue leather jacket is from Banana Republic; and the dresses, Miu Miu. Slim-fit Mark Wong Nark pants are perfect for kicking serious vampire butt. And for storing all her accessories? A Kate Spade bag with bamboo handles.

Off the set, Sarah's style is dependent on her two lives. In other words, the public Sarah Michelle dresses differently from Sarah Gellar, private citizen. When she might be photographed at a premiere or a party, she does designer chic. Laundry is her current favorite, though other top names make the cut as well. She described to a teen magazine, "My style is eclectic. I'm a big fan of Tom Mark, BCBG, Betsey Johnson, Vivienne Tam, and any clothes that are comfortable and kind of funky. I put things together that are a little strange, and when I get tired, my style gets stranger. I love vintage clothes and long leather coats — there's nothing better. You put one on, you always look good. I usually wear skirts. I love that whole knee-length look, which is back now. I love tank tops, summer or winter. I just put a jacket on or a sweater over one." Underwear that's fun to wear comes from Victoria's Secret.

To an evening event, she goes for trendy

stuff like glitter tops, micro-minis, and high boots. Sarah's sparkle comes from within — and from without: "I use body glitter on my shoulders and chest," she's admitted.

Take the spotlight off the girl and it's all different. "I don't like people looking at me. I don't want to walk into a room and have people look at me. I want to look at other people. I'm a baseball hat and overalls girl on the weekends," she once said. She's also, mostly, a natural-look babe. "When I'm not working, I rarely wear makeup. I just put on sunblock, moisturizer, and lip balm." She stashes a black hat in her makeup bag, in case a bad hair day strikes.

Her jewelry is low-key enough for either of her lives. "I love small, delicate things," she told *YM*, adding that she has five holes in her ears and one in her belly button, which she pierced before it got popular.

A dash of vanilla goes wherever Sarah does. "It's my absolute favorite scent," she declared to *People* magazine. "I have vanilla lip balm, vanilla hand lotion, and vanilla essential oil."

## In the Boy Zone

Notoriously private, Sarah doesn't dish about dudes. She won't divulge if there's someone special in her life, but she has talked much about her type. In her early teens, she told *Soap Opera Magazine* she used to be influenced by movies like *Can't Buy Me Love* and *Sixteen Candles.* "I thought I was going to turn sixteen, be the captain of the cheerleading squad, and have some boy knock on my door and say, 'I'm Mr. Wonderful.' I've since realized that's not going to happen."

She began realizing that in her late teens, when she started to date. At seventeen, she divulged, "I'm very outgoing until it comes to actually seeing a guy and meeting him for the first time — then I'm very quiet and I can't think of a word to say and I just go, 'Uh, hmmmmm.'"

She also admitted to a chronic case of bad timing. "I usually meet people in very strange places — like, I met a guy on a train once, only I was on the way to visit another boy."

Another obstacle to romance is maturity levels. Sarah's been around adults most of her life — she can't help feeling that "most of the boys my age are not all that mature," not to mention uncomfortable with her high-profile career. "When I go out with my friends, people [used to] look at me and say, 'There's the girl from *All My Children.*' It makes me uncomfortable."

That was back in 1994. It has to have only gotten worse. "Sometimes," Sarah opined, "guys are put off if you have a job and they don't." Still, back then she preferred dating actors. "A bad day in show business is a lot different from a bad day anywhere else. It takes someone who's been through it to understand."

In spite of the obstacles, Sarah has been in several relationships — enough to spout wisdom and advice. "I think you have to compromise a bit to make relationships work. I mean, I would never change drastically. But I think for two people to get along, you have to have some compromise." As an example, she offered up a personal experience. "I had a boyfriend who smoked, and it just really bothered me. He would smoke constantly, and I asked him and he stopped."

Opposites may attract, but they don't always make for long-lasting relationships, according to Sarah's experience. She told a magazine, "The last guy I went out with was the exact opposite of me. He was like, 'Let's stay home,' and I'd say, 'Let's go out.' He'd say, 'No, there's a nice TV special on.'"

She's come to the conclusion that "you shouldn't be going out with someone just to say you're going out with them. You're going out with them, hopefully, because you enjoy who they are. You have to be true to yourself, and if you're not happy with what you're doing, you've crossed the line."

These days, Sarah is very clear about what she's looking for in a soul mate — or at least a Saturday night date. "Compatibility keeps me interested." And although she told *Rolling Stone,* "I don't really date in the business — so if you know any nice investment bankers . . . ," she has been seen, on at least one occasion, with screenwriter/director Roger Kumble, who just so happens to be directing her newest film.

Sarah says that she would not be anyone's ideal girlfriend right now — "I'm never home. I'm either working or asleep," she told *YM* — but even so, she's admitted to some questionable choices, dumping the "nice, safe boy for the bad boy." Not unlike, she's quick to note, the Buffy-Xander-Angel attraction triangle.

At the end of the day, Sarah's not so sure she even wants to be in a serious relationship. "Like any job, there are sacrifices. Everyone misses having a boyfriend, but [I'm young] and right now, my career comes first."

Does it ever.

# 6

# I Know What You Did . . . and How You *Scream*ed!

In Sarah's case, what she did during hiatus (showbiz speak for vacation) is pretty much a no-brainer. "I'm a workaholic and proud of it," she once declared without apology. "I'm the type of person who gets bored if I don't work for two days. Weekends are boring, anyway." She added that she'd just as soon do a movie if her TV show is on hiatus.

Cool, because the movies are thrilled to have her. And they did, big-time.

In 1997, during her three-month-long *Buffy* break, Sarah managed to squeeze in a double wallop of big-screen gigs. Both were hip horror flicks written by "screen-frighter" supreme Kevin Williamson, both rated R pics became box office bonanzas, and in both our indestructible slayer ended up quite . . . slain!

*I Know What You Did Last Summer* was the more suspenseful of the two. The movie version of the famous young adult novel by Lois Duncan, it's about four friends — Julie, Helen, Ray, and Barry — and the tragic events of a summer night's drive. Sarah described, "Four of us go partying, doing teen stuff . . . fooling around. Nothing serious. Except that on the way home, we hit and kill this guy. And to cover it up, we throw the body in the water."

Who's to know? Well, as the title suggests . . . someone.

That someone is out to torment them. And does, quite successfully.

The cast of *I Know* was a quartet of Hollywood's brightest young stars. Jennifer Love Hewitt, *Party of Five*'s Sarah, starred as Julie. Hotties Ryan Phillippe and Freddie Prinze Jr. were Barry and Ray, respectively.

The part of Helen Shivers went to Sarah, who admitted that she was "thisclose" to turning it down. In an on-line interview, she explained her turnaround. "I assumed the character [a beauty pageant winner] was just another stereotypical dumb blond, but then I realized she had more depth. She's different from the Helen of the original book — a character I would not have played, because she was horribly vain. But in the script, she made a transition. [And I realized] this is a girl whose [sense of identity] was based solely on her looks. All that was expected of her was to be the beautiful girl, to have the perfect boyfriend, and to be a model. And that's what she gave them. But the transition she makes is that by the end, she realizes her looks aren't going to get her through the situation and she's capable of more. Helen makes some wrong choices, she runs up the stairs when she should be running out the door — but she fights back and tries her best to make decisions that might save her."

Still, Sarah remained severely unthrilled with Helen's fashion sense. On-line, she spilled, "I was self-conscious about the outfits. I kept trying to convince [the director] that it should be an evening gown competition and not a bathing suit competition. And I tried to convince them to let me wear pants instead of jeans shorts. But that was my character, and I had to go with it. But it took a lot of coaxing to get me into those outfits."

That aside, Sarah was into the rest of it.

Her decision to go with *I Know* was based on being a horror film buff — and the challenge of playing someone who isn't the Buff.

"It's so unbelievably scary. There's nothing like the adrenaline rush you get [from horror movies]," she said to *YM*. "You know it's fake, that nothing really bad is going to happen, but it's still scary and fun. It's like a roller coaster ride."

Unlike Buffy, who stalks vampires, Helen becomes the stalkee. And Sarah hoped fans got it. "I just hope people watch [*I Know*] for the character and aren't distracted by Buffy. I hope I did a good enough departure that you don't sit there and think, 'Oh, there's Buffy,'" she told *Mr. Showbiz* on-line.

The challenge not to be perceived as Buffy was almost as hard as not playing her TV kick-butt character, who embraces danger. "It was hard to forget my training. I had to put rocks in my shoes and untie my laces and stuff like that," Sarah revealed of her [tricks] to switch personas. "It was a stretch," she conceded.

It was no stretch at all for Sarah and her costars to kick it behind the scenes on the movie's isolated Southport, North Carolina, location. "It was an amazing bonding experience," she said. "The four of us didn't have anybody else down there. There wasn't even a Starbucks. We had one local movie theater and I think it was playing *Tootsie*, first-run."

It helped that she already knew Ryan, who was on daytime's *One Life to Live* when Sarah was on *AMC*. She hung out with him, Freddie Prinze Jr., and Love Hewitt — the girls admitted to being spooked by the town's huge fishermen population.

Sarah conceded that relations between the Hollywood movie crew and the residents of Southport weren't always smooth. In a *Mr. Showbiz* on-line interview, she divulged, "I think the people resented us somehow. They would close restaurants down when they saw us coming. They'd decide to [make noise] when we were filming. But in their defense, it's hard. We monopolized their little town, we were up at weird hours." Still, Sarah and the cast were just as happy to return to the Starbucks-soaked, cosmopolitan climes of Los Angeles.

*I Know What You Did Last Summer* opened in October 1997 with a bang. Not only did the chiller earn great reviews, it topped the box office charts for two weeks running, collecting a cool $70 million.

*    *    *

The day Sarah wrapped *I Know* was the day she started her second film of the summer: *Scream 2*. Being part of this movie was not planned. In fact, it conflicted with her *Buffy* schedule. But when Sarah decides she wants something, she finds a way to make it work, and she *had* to have a piece of *Scream 2*, she confessed in *Entertainment Weekly*. "I so desperately wanted to be a part of this movie, I called my agent and I was like, please, please, please, get me in this movie. It just had a cool feeling about it."

*Scream 2* also had a serious hip-horror pedigree. It was, of course, the sequel to the record-smashing 1996 original *Scream* — the highest-grossing horror picture of all time, raking in $103 million in the U.S. alone.

Cleverly mixing spine-tingling terror with outrageous humor, *Scream 2* revolved around the much-stalked Sidney Prescott, now a freshman at a seemingly serene college in the Midwest. But where Sidney goes, knife-wielding, friend-offing terror follows. And college is no different: The nightmare of *those phone calls*, that *voice*, and all that carnage has begun all over again. As has the race to unmask the real killer.

66

The "surviving" cast of the original *Scream* reassembled for the sequel, including *Party of Five*'s Neve Campbell as Sidney, *Friends'* Courteney Cox as reporter Gale Weathers, David Arquette as Deputy Dewey, and Jamie Kennedy as friend and classmate Randy.

Although Sarah was added to the cast at the last moment and her role was never meant to be much more than a cameo, it was memorable. She played Cici, a chatty sorority sister who, about one-third of the way through the movie, comes too close to the wrong end of the killer's knife and leaps off the sorority house balcony to her death. Before that, however, she manages a funny riff on *Party of Five* — cute because of Neve, of course.

In spite of Sarah's own hip-celeb status, she admitted to moments of intimidation her first day on the *Scream 2* set, especially when she shared an elevator with Neve and David Arquette. Nothing was said until Neve turned around and brightly welcomed her, "You're Sarah, right? Love [Hewitt — Neve's *Po5* costar] said to say hello." From that moment on — in spite of the fact that they had no scenes together — Sarah and Neve became buds.

*Scream 2* turned out to be a worthy successor to the original. It opened on December 12, 1997, to rave reviews, including an *A-* from *Entertainment Weekly* and humongo box office.

After finishing back-to-back horror movies, Sarah was asked if she stressed about being typecast. She didn't. "It's random that I did these two movies in a row. They just offered me the best opportunities to play three-dimensional characters and to do drama, horror, action and comedy combined. That's an actor's dream. So if that's typecasting — I should be so lucky!"

But what, if anything, did Sarah gain from her back-to-back horror movies? New acting techniques? A newfound passion for movies over TV? A deeper understanding of the psychology of terror? Nah. Something much more basic: She earned her PhD in screaming.

"I've learned so much about screaming," she detailed. "You have to do it over and over again. There's the 'I'm being chased' scream, the 'I'm five minutes from freedom' scream, and the 'Oh my God, I'm about to be killed' scream. I screamed my head off!"

**Buffy and Beyond**

When Sarah looks ahead, she has hopes for *Buffy*, her movie career, and, of course, her personal life. Often, they're interrelated. As far as *Buffy* goes, she told *People* magazine, "I want my work to scare you to death. We all love that jolt. It's a natural adrenaline rush. I get all my energy from work. I scream, I yell, I come home, I go to sleep. How many other girls get to release their inner demons for a living?" Contrary to rumors that she wants to leave the show, Sarah asserts, "We're going to keep doing *Buffy* as long as we have good stories to tell. This is a show that needs to go out at its highest point."

What exactly is up for the Buff in seasons to come? Expect the unexpected, is pretty much the motto. The show is constantly evolving, with a revolving door of vampires and other forces of evil to contend with. Although Buffy prevailed in the first two seasons, season three returned with a bang as even more dangerous vampires found the Hellmouth a really hot place to inhabit. Buffy will have to deal with the loss — and possible return — of her love, Angel, and the growing and changing needs of her friends. Sarah's ready for it all.

Naturally, she sees lots of movies in her future. Fresh from her two scare-fest flicks, she told *Teen People,* "I'd [next] like to do a nice movie with happy people, and in daylight."

And yet, her upcoming film doesn't exactly fulfill that goal. Sarah spent the hiatus of 1998 much the same as she did the previous year: filming back-to-back movies.

*Cruel Inventions* is going to shock Sarah's fans who know her only as Buffy, for this role is a total 180 from the wholesome slayer. Sarah plays bad — very, very, worse-than-Kendall bad. Her character, Kathryn Merteuil, is evil incarnate. She lies, steals, cheats, and manipulates people without a shred of remorse. And when she's bent on revenge, watch out. This is one sick puppy of a poor little rich teen.

The plot, in broad strokes, involves a pair of seventeen-year-old stepsiblings, Kathryn and Sebastian, who's played by Sarah's *I Know* costar Ryan Phillippe. Rich, pampered, bored, and self-absorbed, they get their kicks from corrupting other people. Until one comes along who seems uncorruptable — that's when Kathryn bets Sebastian he won't be able to make this girl change. While there are some twists and turns along the road —

and both Kathryn and Sebastian get their comeuppance in the end — this is one film Sarah's TV fans might want to skip.

The other film she made during her 1998 hiatus is somewhat more fan-friendly. *Vanilla Fog* is a romantic comedy about a department store executive—played by Sean Patrick Flannery, who tries to resist his attraction to a young woman he believes has magical powers. She's a chef who finds a way to make magic in the kitchen. That would be Sarah's character.

Acting is what she's always wanted, but it's not all she wants now. Writing has become a goal as well, as she told a journalist. "I would like to write children's stories. It is something I still plan to do. Dr. Seuss is my idol."

Sarah has long put her personal life on the back burner in favor of her career. She plans to keep on doing just that. College — and marriage — will just have to wait. About the former, Sarah once said, "Even if I don't go, I'll continue to take classes, because that's what I really enjoy. I like learning for learning's sake, not necessarily so that I can have a diploma in my hand."

And about a ring on her finger? "As for

marriage, I'll do that, too, but that's far in the future," she predicted.

As for the now: "I want to be working on projects I enjoy. As long as I have material I can sink my teeth into, I will continue to love what I do."

And one more thing: "I don't know if I've taken the time to just sit back and enjoy [my work]. I would like to take a little more time [to do that]."

Nah . . . two more things: "You know what? I'll relax when I'm old!"

# 7

# Nicholas Brendon
# as Xander Harris

*"You have to learn to laugh at life
and not take it too seriously."*

In reel life his character is Alexander Harris, but everyone calls him Xander. In real
life, he's Nicholas Brendon, but his friends
know him as Nicky. Nicky makes friends frequently and easily. He's as outgoing, unaffected, easy to talk to and to get to know as,
well, Xander.

He's also every bit as funny.

"Xander is awkwardly geeky, ugly — so he
has to use his sense of humor," Nicky once
joked. "He's really the funny guy, the one who
reacts to the horrific stuff by tossing off one-

73

liners. The one who shrugs off murders and goes, 'Oh, well, life goes on.'"

In a lot of ways, Xander is much like another TV character, with whom his name sorta rhymes — he's almost a teenage version of *Friends'* Chandler: a guy who doesn't really know how cute and attractive he is and considers himself a flop with girls, even when the evidence is totally to the contrary. No one's more surprised than he when he really does get the girl.

Nicky once said Xander is "the comic relief guy on the show," but that's shortchanging him. A sexy geek, he's way too swoon-worthy for that. In season one, he had a crush on Buffy and at the same time was Willow's not-so-secret crush object. But season two found him actually getting the girl — the unlikeliest of all, snobby, catty Cordelia, the rich in-crowd babe who'd only talk to him one way: down. Even she couldn't help being drawn to Xander's offbeat appeal.

His love life aside, however, Xander is also amazingly brave. He helps Buffy vanquish vampires and assorted demons like he was born to it. When it comes to helping his friends, Xander truly has no fear. Which makes him even hotter.

That Nicky Brendon ended up playing
Xander is truly amazing. Few clues during
his childhood would have suggested it. He
didn't have a lot of money. He didn't start out
as a child actor. He didn't model. He could
barely express himself. But one day, he had
an epiphany: "I don't want to be one of those
guys who's forty years old and never took a
chance. Never tried." Nicky did try — it took
a whole lot of heart, determination, and
courage. He had much to overcome.

## In High School — The Guy Who Never Talked

Nicholas Brendon grew up in Grenada
Hills, a section of Los Angeles' San Fernando
Valley, with his identical twin brother, Kelly;
his baby brothers, Christian and Kyle, and
their parents, Bob and Kathy. As a young
child, Nicky remembers a fairly normal childhood. He went to public school, played Little
League, and occasionally got into twin trouble trying to fool teachers by switching
classes with his brother. He wasn't the best
student but he liked science and English, especially reading. "My favorite books when I
was a kid were anything by C.S. Lewis and
Shel Silverstein's *The Giving Tree*. I loved

that one." His passion was sports, especially baseball.

Even though his mom worked sporadically as a theatrical agent, neither Nicky nor Kelly ever considered a career in acting. They were normal, everyday boys next door. If Nicky had a "when I grow up" goal, it was a toss-up between pro baseball and medicine. Showbiz wasn't in the picture.

Which isn't to say Nicky didn't love making people laugh. Entertaining others gave him a kick. The kick grew into a passion as he grew older. "I was starting to feel the *need* to somehow entertain people," he admitted in an interview. With increasing frequency, he'd try out jokes on his family, say outrageous things just to get a reaction — and it worked. He found he really had a knack for it. But the idea of a career in comedy or acting was too terrifying to even contemplate back then. He relates, "When I was alone with my family, I was fine — I was funny and things were great. It was when I was out in the world . . . Well, people are very judgmental."

Nicky's tough time, when he felt people judged him harshly, was in high school. He went to Chatsworth High, part of the L.A. Unified system — where one of his classmates was Leonardo DiCaprio. But where Leo's admitted to being a class clown, Nicky was the opposite of the guy who goofed off and provided giggles in school. Why? "When I was in high school, I was so insecure, I wouldn't even talk to people. I had a stutter — a horrible stutter that made talking to people hard, and talking in front of people impossible."

"People," of course, included girls. "I never dated at all," Nicky confesses. "I was too shy. At one point, I was really into this good friend of mine, but I was too shy to tell her." Things seemed to slide further downhill during that time and just after those rough high-school years. He didn't feel he was good-looking; zits seemed to pop up at the worst possible times. He fractured his elbow and quit baseball. His studies weren't going so well — his early dream of medicine was becoming ever more distant.

And then his parents broke up.

In a roundabout way, however, dealing with all the bad stuff is what brought him to the happiest time in his life. Facing things head-on — and a talk with God — is what led him to acting. There's no trace of the wisecracking Xander when Nicky tells of the moment that changed his life: "I was sitting in the Jacuzzi in the backyard of our old house. It was summertime, really beautiful, the end of the day with the sun going down. The Dodgers were playing; I had the radio on in the background. And it all hit me. My parents were getting divorced. High school was almost over. What was I going to do? Not baseball, because I quit. And I was just talking to God and I said, 'What can I do?'"

Two thoughts came to him. One, he loved entertaining people — even if it was only in the privacy of his own home, among family who accepted him. And two, he wanted to help his mother out financially. Showbiz seemed like a path.

But there was the stutter. How could he audition for parts, act out a scene, be funny? At this point, most people would have given into that sinking feeling and said, "Forget it. I can't." But Nicky Brendon isn't most people. In a life-changing moment, and not without a lot of courage, he made a decision. "I just came to this conclusion that when I'm forty, I don't want to say, 'I wish I had done that.' So I said, 'You know what? Let's do it.'"

What he meant was, let's work on eliminating the stutter, the one thing that was holding him back. "It was very hard," Nicky admitted in an interview. "I didn't go to a speech therapist. I just did a lot of tongue twisters. I slowed down my speech a lot. It was a lot of hard work. I was happy I did it, though."

Happy and, though it would take seven years (!), eventually successful. Once Nicky felt confident enough, he started lining up acting auditions (with his mom as his agent). Auditions, of course, only get you in the door. Once in front of the casting director, he had to make it on his own. And just like any new-comer to the biz, he piled up lots of rejections before snagging his first gig: a commercial for Clearasil.

Other commercials followed, but only sporadically. In the meantime, he sharpened his acting chops via little-seen stage roles in local L.A. productions. He was in *The Further Adventures of Tom Sawyer, My Own Private Hollywood,* and *Out of Gas on Lover's Leap.*

Doing theater was great experience, but it didn't pay the rent. Like most people who aren't independently wealthy, Nicky needed to make a living. So while he chased down auditions, he did the odd-job thing as a handyman, an electrician, a waiter, and even a messenger. "I tried everything," he conceded.

It was one of those nonacting jobs, however, that led to his first break.

Nicky toiled behind the scenes in the way unglamorous position of production assistant on the TV comedy *Dave's World*. It didn't last long. "They fired me because I was just too darn attractive — they were threatened by me!" Nicky jokes, but that was because casting directors on that show realized he'd be better in front of the camera. "You should be acting," is what they told him just before awarding him a cameo. It led, finally, to more roles.

He had a bit part in the movie *Children of the Corn, Part III* and nailed guest spots on such TV shows as *The Young and the Restless* and *Married . . . With Children*.

And then came the Buffster.

## *Buffy the Vampire Slayer*: "Five Days That Changed My Life"

By the time Nicky found out about the auditions for *Buffy the Vampire Slayer*, he was no longer a client of his mom's. In fact, he wasn't an acting client of anyone's. He was a waiter. Correction: an out-of-work waiter, since he'd just broken his elbow in a sports-related accident. He had just started seeing a girl and was at her house recuperating, when out of the blue, she said, "If you ever want to act, let me know." It turned out that her mother was also an agent, and she clued Nicky in about the *Buffy* auditions. He went for it.

"Everything happened quickly," Nicky relates. "When I first went in and read for it, the show wasn't even a show. It wasn't even a pilot. It was a presentation." Nicky must have done something right, even at that very early stage. "I had a callback," he remembers, "and met Joss [Whedon]. The next day I tested at Fox [the production company] and on the weekend, I tested for the WB network. Tuesday I got the call — I'd booked it. So in all, it was five days that changed my life."

Like the rest of the cast, Nicky dove right into the show. "We filmed thirteen episodes before any ever aired, so we had no way of knowing, when we were working, how people would react to the show. So there was a lot of impatience, a lot of being nervous. But in our hearts, we knew it was good because Joss is an amazing writer." He adds, "Our show is fun and entertaining — and the timing is right."

## What He's Really, Really Like

Naturally, Nicky's often asked for his take on Xander, and what characteristics, if any, he shares with his TV alter ego. His first response — to that and nearly every other question — is a joke. "He's kind of goofy and a wise guy. I'm not as pathetic." But after a while, he gets serious. "Xander has a lot of love to give," he says quietly. "He's the kind of kid who deals with his insecurity by trying to make people laugh. It's a way to keep himself aloof, to not let anybody get that close to him, really. I relate to Xander's sense of humor. I love the fact that he's funny, has emotions, and he's insecure."

Nicky is more complex than Xander. Yes, he's funny, but he's intensely introspective. When things aren't going well, he likes to be alone with his thoughts, "sitting on my balcony in my rocking chair and looking at the Hollywood Hills. The lights of L.A. are spread out below me."

In fact, Nicky prefers spending off-time at

home, as opposed to making the party scene. Of course, his new digs, which he shares with his brother Kelly, are da bomb. (He even invited the magazine *In Style* in for a fact and photo session.) Flush with *Buffy* success, he bought a 1920s Spanish-style duplex way up in the Hollywood Hills. So far up, in fact, that he climbs fifty-three steps to get to his front door!

Always decor-obsessed, Nicky furnished it with all his favorite furniture and antiques, many picked up on the cheap at garage sales. Among his treasures: an old dentist's cabinet from the 1850s with twelve drawers. Stripped and refinished, it functions as Nicky's desk.

"I'm a huge rocking chair fan," he reveals, and his home boasts five of them. Most used is a springy vintage chair, upholstered in velvet. He's got a natural pine sleigh bed, but no bedroom door: A burgundy curtain hangs in the doorway. He painted all the walls himself, periwinkle in the dining room and beige in his office.

Lately, Nicky's gotten into reading bigtime. On his bookshelf these days: classics by Ernest Hemingway and lots of mysteries. He also watches lots of old movies, but not just for enjoyment; that's one way Nicky studies acting techniques.

Music is always blasting around him, whether he's home, in the car, or in his dressing room. You never know what you'll hear — it could be anything from classical to jazz, blues, alternative, or rock. On his CD player, Ella Fitzgerald and Frank Sinatra spin next to Nerf Herder and Cake. A portrait of jazz great Louis Armstrong hangs in his living room.

On weekends, he looks for pickup softball and basketball games or plans camping and hiking trips with his buds. His closest bud is his twin brother, Kelly, who lives with him. Kelly's a fledgling actor who's currently, as Nicky puts it, "pounding the pavement."

Kelly and Nick not only look alike and share a love for acting, they're also similar personality-wise. "We both have great senses of humor," Nicky says. Fans often mistake Kelly for Nicky and ask for an autograph. Both brothers are cool with it. "He'll call me up," Nick relates, "and say, 'Nick, we got recognized again.' But people who really know us never confuse us."

Nicky's remained tight with his entire family. He sees his mom and younger brothers all the time, and his dad calls once a week, "mostly on Monday nights, to comment on the show."

While Xander has become a true believer, Nicky is not into vampires — he's never even read an Anne Rice book. "I don't believe any exist like we see them on the show. If I was the kind of person who was into that, I think I'd be spending lots of time in computer chat rooms, talking to other people who feel the same way." As it is, he doesn't even own a computer. Humbly, he confesses, "Before *Buffy* came along, I couldn't even afford one."

## Girlfriends: "Looks Don't Matter to Me"

He might have been too shy to date in high school, but Nicky has apparently made up for lost time. He met his last girlfriend at a pickup softball game in a local park. She pitched, he played shortstop.

In spite of that, Nicky insists that sometimes he feels as insecure as he did as a young teenager. "I don't see myself as being cute, or hot," he revealed in an interview, adding, "I get tongue-tied when I talk to a girl I like. I'm all jittery and I say stupid things, which pretty much ensures I'll never date her!"

The kind of girl he'd like to date has to have two qualities: "A sense of humor — and strong hands for giving back rubs! Strange as it sounds, looks don't matter to me." Nicky's idea of a great date involves a couple of bottles of Snapple and good conversation.

Being recognized by fans is something new in his life that he really gets a kick out of. "To me, signing autographs is new and I like it." Nicky has strong feelings of appreciation toward his fans. As he told a journalist, "When you're an actor, you have an unsigned contract [with the fans]. If I buy a house in the Hills, it's my fans and the people who enjoy my work that helped me buy that house. So, if I go out to dinner with my girlfriend, my wife — or one of my five wives! — you have to sign the autograph. They're very important to your career. You have to say, 'Thank you very much,' and sign that piece of paper. But it's more than an obligation. I mean, it's great! People are giving you accolades — how could you not like that?"

"Of course," he concedes, "there are some inappropriate times for people to come up to you, but when you go out into a social environment, you have to deal with it."

## "I Want to Inspire People"

Where does Nicky see himself in the next few years? For the immediate future, careerwise, it's the *Buff*. "I love being on the show. It's so amazing, so well written. It's like a movie every week." Speaking of which, Nicky would like to do movies someday. But he's choosy about what kind. "I'd like to stay away from the horror genre," he admitted to a magazine. "I don't want to get typecast. One of my favorite actors, Anthony Perkins, did *Psycho* and after that, everyone saw him only as [the character he played] Norman Bates."

Instead, Nicky dreams of doing small independent films. "That's where you can really play a nice part. Eventually, down the road, I'd like to write and direct — be on both sides of the camera at the same time. But for now, I'm the luckiest guy in Hollywood."

Nicky has goals beyond his own career. "I want to inspire people," he says. "I want people to say, 'Nicholas Brendon, he's supposedly the nicest guy in the world.' I want to do good work, but more than that, I want to stay a good human being. That's more important than any character I play."

Nicky has a message for *Buffy*'s fans. It comes from his own life experience. "I just kind of developed my sense of humor through a life full of ups and downs. You just have to learn to laugh at life and not take it so seriously. Never lose the inner child in you. And remember, there's nothing that you can't do. If you *want* to do it, you've *got* to do it."

# 8

# Alyson Hannigan
# as Willow Rosenberg

### *"Buffy Is Who You Want to Be—but Willow Is Who Most People Are"*

Willow Rosenberg has always been many things to many people. To the snobby popular crowd at Sunnydale High, she was someone to mock, because she cared more about computers than about being one of them.

To Buffy Summers, Willow has been a loyal best bud from the day the teen slayer hit town.

To Xander Harris, she's always been someone to depend on, a friend for life who not-so-secretly pined for him — even when he fell for Buffy.

To Cordelia Chase, she was Willow who? At first, Willow wasn't even on Cordelia's radar screen.

So goes the back story, anyway. But what a difference a few hit seasons make. Now Willow has blossomed from shy wallflower to clever, confident cyberchick, able to solve undead mysteries with a single click. She's also moved beyond unrequited crushing to being with someone who loves her right back.

Through it all, Willow has stayed true to herself. She was always okay with the "computer nerd" tag; she pretty much accepted her basically bashful vibe. In fact, Willow considers herself lucky. She's always had what most high-school kids are still looking for: great friends and the gift of knowing what she loves to do — computers and teaching. But Willow's most amazing trait is her unflinching ability to focus on the positive and, no matter what, never let the jerks get her down. She's the über-best friend.

It's inconceivable to think of anyone else playing Willow. Alyson Hannigan is softly pretty, megatalented, and infuses her character with just the right balance of social klutziness and cool confidence. Even back in her nerdiest days, Willow has always been kinda cool.

## A McDonald's Moppet

Of all the *Buffy* stars, Alyson is the one who can match Sarah Michelle Gellar in years of experience bouncing the showbiz boards. Like her TV best bud, Alyson began in her single-digit years — in her case, that would be age four. That's when the Washington, D.C.-born, Atlanta-bred kid started appearing in TV commercials. Practically the same time Sarah was gobbling Whoppers for Burger King, Alyson was pitching patties for rival fast-food chain McDonald's. She also honed her shilling skills in ads for Six Flags amusement parks and Oreo cookies.

In an on-line interview, Alyson explained, "It actually started because both of my parents were photographers. When I was a baby, I would model for them. So that's what led into commercials."

Her parents may have gotten the ball rolling, but what led her from commercials to an actual acting career was her own inner motivation and talent. Alyson admitted, "It's always felt right to be in front of the camera.

I was the kid who wanted to be Cindy Brady when I watched *The Brady Bunch.*"

Alyson was always a creative kid. She used to believe her toys had secret lives and would spend hours trying to "catch them at it," as she confessed in an on-line chat.

When Alyson was eleven, she moved with her mom from Atlanta to Los Angeles, where her kiddie career kicked into higher gear. Roles came regularly, on screens both large and small. She played Dan Aykroyd and Kim Basinger's daughter in the movie comedy *My Stepmother Is an Alien.* She couldn't know it at the time, but one of her costars on that movie would eventually be one of her costars on *Buffy* — Seth Green!

Alyson's early TV credits include guest gigs on *Picket Fences, Roseanne,* and *Touched by an Angel.* She earned recurring roles in two pre-Buffster series, both short-lived efforts. *Almost Home* was the renamed *Torkelsons,* memorable mostly because of Alyson's costars: Brittany Murphy (Tai in the movie *Clueless*) and Jason Marsden (*Boy Meets World*). The other show was 1989's *Free Spirit,* which was about a witch hired as a housekeeper for a widower and three kids.

Alyson clearly worked a lot during her teen

years and met many young acting peers, but she was not exactly a household name. While others (such as Brittany Murphy, Jason Marsden, Melissa Joan Hart) were hitting it big, she continued to snag only bit parts, or roles in shows that weren't on very long.

But she didn't really mind. In an important sense, the pacing of her career worked well. It allowed her to keep up a normal school life. After her high-school graduation, she enrolled in college, where she toyed with switching directions and going into psychology or possibly zoology. "I love animals, so any work like that would have been good." But she came to the conclusion that, at the end of the day, "My real ambition was acting."

Good thing, too, because her big break — *Buffy the Vampire Slayer* — was right around the corner.

## "I Think Fans Know More About Me Than I Do!"

Alyson insists that auditioning for the Willow role was "nerve-racking." It isn't unusual for an actor to be called back several times to re-audition for the same part, but in Alyson's case, the tryouts totals were over-the-top. "I auditioned nine times," she revealed on-line.

"It was a process of elimination — a nerve-racking process! Finally, just as the suspense was killing me, they gave me the job."

As if it could have gone to anyone else. Alyson candidly confesses that she and her character totally get each other — and so do most viewers. "I love Willow. If I could choose which character to play, I would choose Willow. People really relate to her. Buffy is who you [might] want to be — but Willow is who most people are. It's nice being so real."

In an interview with *Teenbeat* magazine, Alyson elaborated on the connection with her character. "Like Willow, I focus on the positive, but I'm not as smart as she is. She's really bookwormy wise, computer literate. I can make my way around the Internet, but I can't hack into a computer system like she can."

Alyson also claims to share an offbeat sense of humor with Willow. "We might be the only two laughing at the same jokes," she conceded, in answer to a fan's question.

Alyson might add that, like Willow, she's unassuming, basically shy—and totally okay with it. Of all the cast members, she's done the least amount of self-promotion or publicity. Magazines don't run lots of interviews with her, and her on-line presence is pretty much limited to fan-run sites. She does surf the Net to check out those sites and finds it amazing. "I think they know more about me than I do," she cracked last year.

However, fans can expect to see more of Alyson soon. She recently hired a publicist, and posed bare-backed for a Jansport backpack ad, which was *really* cool!

## At Home — Not Alone

There are other ways in which reel life and real life intersect. The Alyson you might meet on the street doesn't look appreciably different from Willow. For one thing, they kinda dress alike. "I have the best clothes on the show," Alyson asserts. "Leave the short skirts to Buffy. I'm the fuzzy, huggable one." For another, they're both unfailingly nice and polite.

When she leaves the *Buffy* set for the day, Alyson heads to her Los Angeles home. It's pretty much decorated in Beanie Baby chic! "I've collected forty-six of them in two years," she revealed in one of her rare magazine interviews. Her favorite is Bongo the monkey.

Virtual pets are only part of the Hannigan menagerie. Alyson also lives with cats and a dog. The latter needs to be kept far from the Beanie Babies. "I have to keep them out of reach of the dog; he'd like to tear their heads off," Alyson told *In Style* magazine.

What does she do when she's not working? "I like sports," she mentioned on-line, "especially soccer, and anything outdoors. I like playing with my dog. And that's about the only thing I have time to do!"

She also likes going out to the movies — especially horror movies. "I'm a chicken, but I like them. I'm like, any arm next to me is mine to squeeze. I really enjoyed *Scream*. I loved being able to laugh and scream at the same time."

Alyson admits that even her social life parallels Willow's. Back in season one, when Willow didn't have a boyfriend, Alyson said, "I am like her because she doesn't get all the guys, she isn't most popular, she's just kind of in her own little world, crushing on guys who don't have crushes back on her." But now that Willow's happily hooked up with Oz, Alyson has a sweetie in her life as well. So far, private Alyson hasn't publicly revealed her boyfriend's name, but she has implied that she's in a serious relationship.

## "This Is a Great Time for Me"

All the young stars of *Buffy* candidly confess they'd like to transform their small-screen success into big-screen features. Sarah, of course, was the first person to make that leap and Alyson was second. She was most recently in the rated R dark comedy *Dead Man on Campus*, which stars Mark-Paul Gosselaar. "I played Lucy, the dumb one!" Alyson giggled to a teen magazine. "She doesn't have much to do, but she's funny, I hope, and she's in the entire movie. It was an all right little part."

As for her *Buffy* future, Alyson doesn't really know what's up for her TV alter ego, though she has very definite ideas about where she'd like to see it go: She wants Willow to come out of her shell more. "I like the fact that she's become more aggressive." At the end of season two, Willow was supposed to speak up for herself more, "but that part got cut," Alyson groused on-line, adding, "I was very hurt about that."

Season three found her even more firmly together with her steady sweetie, Oz — a definite up side. "The relationship with Oz is so fun," Alyson admits, "and, hopefully, that will continue. I love working with Seth. And I like exploring that boyfriend aspect. I hope we have more kissing scenes!"

Alyson adds, "I think Willow will always love Xander, though."

Speaking of Xander, Nicholas is the cast member who's accompanied Alyson to several sci-fi conventions, where they get to interface with fans in the real world (as opposed to cyberspace). Alyson thinks they'll do more of those, adding, "They're usually a lot of fun." Another venue the usually private Alyson is happy to make an appearance at is a charity fund-raiser. Recently, she and David Boreanaz played pool in a celeb-studded event to benefit AIDS Project L.A.

All in all, everything she's doing right now, on- and off-screen, is über-cool. "This is a great time for me," Alyson concludes. Willow Rosenberg would press the save key on that one!

# 9
# David Boreanaz as Angel

*"I've Never Looked at Myself as a Famous Person — I Probably Never Will"*

Another TV'er might own the name, but no show — or its audience — has really been "touched by an Angel" these past two seasons more than *Buffy the Vampire Slayer.* This otherworldly being, naturally, is the hunky and mysterious, brooding and tortured Angel, totally the first 242-year-old sex symbol TV has ever had!

Over the course of *Buffy*'s run so far, Angel's been through lots of changes. At first, the vampire with a soul lurked in the shadows, acting as the young slayer's omnipresent protector — the spirit who put her on vampire alert. Then, his undead life became even more complicated when he and the Buff fell for each other in a deep, meaningful way. Consider the complications: A vampire in love with a vampire slayer.

But things got even more tangled when the old gypsy curse that had given him a soul in the first place got reversed. That's when Angel reconnected with his inner demon and gleefully tried to off everyone in Buffy's life — including her. The end of season two found Angel reformed, but . . . oops, too late. In order to save the world, Buffy gave Angel one last kiss, then sent him to purgatory, which he didn't emerge from until well into season three.

If the character Angel is by turns mysterious, tortured, brooding, and sexy, the actor who plays him, David Boreanaz, is pretty much none of the above — except, of course, for the crush-worthy part.

Do he and Angel share any qualities at all? David divulges only one: "I'm passionate about what I do, and so is Angel."

## "I Was Obsessed with Football — and Inspired by Theater"

Picking out pictures of David Boreanaz as a little kid could be tricky. He doesn't look much like the hottie the TV-watching world has come to swoon over. "As a kid, I had long, curly blond hair," David related to an on-line fan. "It got darker as I got older, but if I let it grow now, it would still be very curly."

The ringletted rascal grew up in Philadelphia, Pennsylvania, the only son and youngest child of a travel agent mom and WPVI-TV weatherman Dave Roberts (that's his professional name). Following in Dad's footsteps was never little David's dream, however. The boy had two goals in life but only one he felt comfortable enough to tell people about. That would be football.

Naturally athletic David was practically to the gridiron born. He played Peewee League from the time he was really young and dreamed of going pro as soon as he could. "I was obsessed with it, it was all I wanted to do. I drank tons of milk and ate green beans because I heard that made you run faster and jump higher," David divulged to *Twist* magazine.

Whether it was from the nutrition or just raw talent and the willingness to work hard, David excelled at the sport. At Melvern Prep, he played wide receiver and defensive back. He also ran track. Unfortunately, it was the latter sport that dashed his hopes of going pro in the first one: During his junior year, he injured his knee in a track jump. At that moment, "I realized football wasn't going to be the career for me."

David was down, big time. But he wasn't out. Instead of brooding about the career that wasn't to be, he turned to his second passion, the one he felt just as strongly about but had kept hidden: acting. "I was seven years old when my parents took me to see a live performance of *The King and I*, starring Yul Brynner," David has related. "I was inspired by Yul Brynner's performance. The show blew me away. That's why I knew I wanted to be an actor. Right after that, I just wanted to see plays and musicals." Luckily, his parents took him all the time.

Why did he feel the need to keep his nascent love for acting under wraps? David has no real answer to that. "I just would never tell anyone," he admitted. "It was weird. When I'd hit the field, it was football. But behind closed doors, it was theater."

High school was a mixed bag for David emotionally. On the one hand, he was a jock — part of the macho, popular crowd. He was also something of a local celebrity, due to his dad's TV job. "In high school, the players hated me if it rained," he joked to *Seventeen* magazine. "They would razz me, like my dad made it rain on purpose."

But high school presented its share of problems for David in other ways. Physically, he felt more awkward than awesome. "It was a trying period for me," he once revealed. "You know, you have all these hormones racing inside of you. You don't know where you're going. You're stepping left when you should be stepping right. Things are growing on you that you haven't seen growing there before. It's embarrassing, it's frightening."

One of David's most embarrassing moments happened on a high-school date. "I went to the bathroom and realized I had this huge rip right in the seat of my pants!"

David admits to using cover-up tactics for doofy behavior around girls. "I'd bail myself out by doing something totally physical and stupid. I'd spill a glass of water, get up from the table, and take the tablecloth with me. I'd go for any cheap laugh to break the tension."

After his high-school graduation, David enrolled in Ithaca College, in upstate New York. The school is famous for its theater department, and that was David's major. During his four years there, he was in several college productions and in regional theater, too, including the plays *Hatful of Rain* and *Fool for Love.*

When he graduated, he decided to move to Hollywood to try his luck there. He had his parents' blessing. His dad even drove cross-country with him. But Hollywood did not exactly welcome him with open arms. David's "dues-paying days" were long and hard. Under the listing "odd jobs to pay the rent," David painted houses, parked cars, and even handed out towels at a sports club. For a while, the closest he came to a showbiz gig was working behind the scenes in a props department.

Finally, the auditions he went on began to pay off. He did a lot of commercials. "I also did a music video. I was in the chorus, in the background," David reveals. He appeared in the TV movie *Men Don't Lie,* but playing Kelly's biker boyfriend on *Married . . . With Children* was his only series TV credit prior to *Buffy.* That was back in 1993!

When things weren't moving fast enough, David got creative. As he explained in *Entertainment Weekly,* he crashed studio gates, literally attempting to "break in" to the biz. "I'd put on a suit and pretend I was an executive just to get into studio lots. I'd pass out résumés and talk to people." Did it work? Not even. "I was in this one agency and I had security chasing me around the building," he laughed.

But in the end, it was plain old random luck — being in the right place at the right time — that led him to the *Buffy* studio lot, this time as a paid cast member.

## Props to the Pooch

"If it wasn't for Bertha Blue, I probably wouldn't have gotten the part of Angel," David told a reporter. Who's Ms. Blue? She's not a casting director, nor an agent, manager, or talent scout. At the time, in fact, she was only three years old. Bertha Blue is David's dog. "She's a pound dog, a Lab mix with a little greyhound in her. I rescued her when she was a pup," he says.

He was playing with his pup in a Hollywood park in 1996 when a talent manager spotted him and asked him if he was an actor. Honestly, David admitted that he'd only done a few commercials so far, plus the solo gig on *Married . . . With Children*. The manager gave David his card and offered to represent him.

David took him up on the offer. Good move. Not long after, David auditioned for the role of Angel. "The whole thing happened very fast," he's said. "I didn't even have an entire script to read, just eight pages." Clearly, David rocked those pages, because he booked the role the next day. There was only one caveat: He wasn't a regular cast member. At first, Angel was just a recurring character, signed for only seven episodes out of *Buffy*'s initial thirteen in season one. But fate — well, more like fans — changed all that. After a few appearances, Angel became the most buzzed-about character on the show — via snail mail from fans and Web sites from the cyberconnected.

The producers were listening. By season two he was promoted to a full-fledged regular. Not that there was anything remotely regular about that season. That's when Buffy and Angel began acting on their mutual attraction. Lots of smooching ensued, although it was trippy: During their first kiss, Angel lost control and sprouted fangs. The second time Buffy accidentally burned him with her crucifix. Eventually, they got it together, but their final declaration of adoration led to bad things. Angel's one true moment of happi-

ness, bummer, led to his becoming soul-
challenged once again.

## "People Don't Know What to Make of Me — Good Guy, or Vampire?"

Both, actually. Especially through the first
two seasons, no one knew Angel's true colors
for sure. No wonder — the dude morphed
from mysterious stalker to angelic lover to
killer and back again. What might have con-
fused and frustrated fans, however, is what
psyched David. The versatility of the role is
what he grooves on most. "Angel is just a good
guy in a bad situation," David told *TV Guide*
back in 1997. "But it's an amazing role. To
play a 242-year-old vampire with a con-
science, you can go in a lot of directions.
What's a blessing about this character is that
I can really exercise my chops. I want him to
stay well-balanced."

Angel also stays active. His fight scenes (on
behalf of the Buffster, or against her) are nu-
merous, as are his stunts. "I've been doing a
lot of my own stunts," David told an on-line
fan. He draws the line at falling through win-
dows, though, wisely leaving that stuff to the
pros.

107

## Angel in the Sunlight: What He's Really Like

David's entire life may have changed when he became Angel, but *he* hasn't changed at all. The same sweet, decent, friendly guy he always was, David is in no danger of an ego swell. "I've never looked at myself as a famous person," he said recently. "I probably never will. In fact, it's kind of a strange word, 'famous.' I always just want to be a regular person, remember my roots, where I came from." He doesn't even think he's all that good-looking. "If people could only see my pictures from college . . ." he muses about his heartthrob status.

When the cameras stop rolling, David starts rocking. He's always in motion, whether it's swinging at virtual golf balls with a virtual club or pantomiming kicks, spins, and karate moves. He loves being outdoors and is totally sports-obsessed, playing hockey, baseball, tennis, skiing, and actual golf when he can or, if not, watching it on TV. He'd love to add basketball to that already long list, but somehow, "my knee always pops out," he complained in an on-line interview. Though he's naturally athletic, he does have to work out to stay in shape and goes to the gym regularly. "I'm into boxing now," he divulged.

David loves to stay on the cutting edge of trendy sports. His idea of what's on the envelope? Bowling. "Everyone's discovered golf," he told *In Style* magazine, "but bowling is next. It's totally on its way back."

When he does manage to stay in one place, it's often with a book. "I have a library of tons of authors that I read. I often read three or four books at the same time." He'll read anything to do with film, from biographies (Marlon Brando is the most current one he's read) to dramas by Tennessee Williams, to children's authors who've also written adult books, such as Roald Dahl and Dr. Seuss, to self-help books. "My father turned me on to Og Mandino when I was in grade school; he kind of gave me books for inspiration."

Far from his brooding TV persona, up close and in person David has a sunny disposition and is always smiling. He's upbeat to the max — deliberately so. In fact, seeing the positive side of any situation is pretty much his philosophy. "I'm not going to be miserable in a miserable situation," he declared in a revealing on-line interview. "[Instead, I always think] 'How can I turn this around?' Because

I know [whatever the situation is] it's temporary. So why hurt yourself even more? I mean, there are times when, yeah, you're like, 'This is the pits, man, this is terrible.' And you get depressed. But you've got to remind yourself that this is temporary, and then you just go and make the best of it."

It was the reaction to him on the Internet that first gave producers a clue about Angel's popularity. David remains the cast member to boast the most sites devoted to him, including the aptly named "Angel's Shrine of Drool."

"It's freaky sometimes," David admits about the cyber outpouring of emotion for him, but mostly, he feels blessed to have so many fans. He takes as much time as possible not only to write back, but every once in a while, to surprise a fan with a phone call. "At first, they don't believe it's me," he admitted to a reporter, until he quotes from the fan's letter to him.

Unsurprisingly, David has always been a chick magnet. When quizzed about his "type," he answered, "Intelligence is very sexy. I like girls I can have a real conversation with about music, poetry and great books — but who can laugh and have fun, just go for burgers and hang out in a playground."

However, David's dating days are officially over. Quietly and privately, he married his longtime girlfriend, Ingrid, in the spring of 1998. They met at a party nearly four years ago. "She was looking for a place to sit down and I offered her my chair. We've been together ever since," David told *Seventeen*. The necklace he wears on *Buffy*, and the Claddagh ring Angel gave Buffy are actually his own, given to him by Ingrid. The latter is his most precious piece of jewelry. David describes its meaning: "The heart represents the love, and the hands are the friendship."

## The Future: Touched by This Angel

So what's coming up for the hottest "undead" dude on TV? Aside from his swoony return to the Buffster, there are exciting plans afoot. David has signed to star in his own show. It'll be called *Angel*, and it is scheduled to air on the WB network starting in the fall of 1999.

While he's über-pumped about that, like most consummate actors, David doesn't want to be confined to just TV. He sees the movies in his future as well. "It's like two different kinds of paint on a canvas, oil and water. Both are beautiful." Making his mark on the big screen would hopefully include writing, producing, and directing, as well as acting. His dream role? Spider-Man.

He doesn't dismiss an eventual return to the stage, either. In fact, David believes in doing theater, for any actor. "It makes you feel confident," he advises.

In both his personal and professional life, David is completely psyched by the way things are going. He takes none of it for granted, promising, "I just have to count my blessings and work hard."

# 10

# Charisma Carpenter
# as Cordelia Chase

## *"Cordelia Is Glamorous, Sexy, Forward — and Nothing Like Me"*

Over the course of Buffy's run, all the main characters have grown and changed. None more so, however, than Cordelia Chase. "Cordy," as she's sometimes called, practically did a 180, personality-wise. She started off as little more than a one-dimensional cardboard *Clueless* refugee — more a stereotype than a person. She was the stuck-up ice princess who existed mainly to torment Buffy and her buds, while representing the arrogant popular clique.

At first, Cordelia was a recurring, rather than a regular cast member. But by the end of season one, the part grew — in a wholly unexpected way. First, she fell into a smoochy relationship with Xander, previously the object of her scorn. When she suddenly got that she really liked him, Cordy renounced her snobbish ways — and, to the delight of the actress who plays her, earned her "stake" as a slayerette.

## "Yes, It *Is* My Real Name"

Charisma Carpenter totally sounds like a made-up stage name. Surprise: It isn't. The youngest child and only daughter of Chris and Don Carpenter, she didn't even *have* a name for her first few days, until her mother was inspired by the name of a bottle of perfume. Charisma explains, "My grandmother really loved Avon perfume and she brought this bottle to my mom. My mom thought it was horrible — the stinkiest thing she'd ever smelled in her life. But . . . she loved the name. So I was named after a tacky bottle of perfume from Avon." Charisma is another word for magnetic charm.

Think growing up with such an unusual name would be cool? Think again. According to Charisma, it was "a curse, an absolute curse," she blurted to a roomful of TV critics, adding that *she* didn't like the perfume, either. "It was nasty."

In elementary school, teachers didn't even try to pronounce it. "When they were taking attendance the first day of school, it would be like . . . 'uh . . . is there a Carpenter in the room?' And kids would come up to me and say, 'Charisma? What's that, a disease?'"

For a time, she compensated, calling herself Chrissy. Her mother, of all people, was not amused. "There's only one Chris in this family, and it's me," Mom would remind her.

Charisma — pronounced, by the way, Ca-*riz*-ma — is a native of Las Vegas, Nevada, a city she insists is "more normal than people imagine." Not that she had a particularly typical childhood. For starters, she was often entered in kiddie beauty pageants, courtesy of Mom, a former pageant participant herself. Charisma didn't mind being on the circuit. She didn't feel pressured to look a certain way, and actually gained a lot of self-confidence from those days. "My mom had a real healthy attitude about it," she shared with a reporter. "So it was a positive experience for me."

She attended private parochial school and started ballet lessons. The latter would quickly become her passion. As she told

*Jump* magazine, "By the time I was nine, I was going to local hotels entertaining the guests. I would do it with my cousins — Patty was the comedian, my other cousin Judy was the singer, and I was the dancer. We performed every weekend." Those lessons, combined with rehearsals every weekday, were majorly labor intensive. "I wasn't like most kids in that I didn't get home from school and watch cartoons and eat and do my homework. I went to ballet and got home around nine P.M. Then, I'd do my homework, go to bed, and go to school the next day."

Elementary school was not a comfortable place. Her outsider status was sealed because of her weird name, reinforced by her weird fashion sense. "My mom owned a store," she told an interviewer, "and I'd dress in things she sold, like satin pants, when no one else was wearing them."

When Charisma was thirteen, everything changed — starting with her family's move to a small Mexican town south of Rosarito. She didn't attend a neighborhood school but commuted daily to not one, but *two* different schools. Both were in the U.S. — in just-over-the-border Chula Vista, outside San Diego, California. She explained, "I went to one

116

school for academics, then I'd take a bus to a magnet school that specialized in the arts — music, dance, theater."

Charisma claims she didn't fit in at either school — but it was definitely worse at the academically oriented one. "It was very social-statusy, people were judged by the clothes they wore, and the kind of car their families had. It wasn't that I didn't have cute clothes, but these weren't things I cared about. I was into ballet, I was into my friends and my boyfriends."

At the Chula Vista School of the Arts, however, things were somewhat better. At least there all the students were into some form of the arts, and Charisma remained bent on ballet: She'd never stopped taking lessons and had pretty much planned on going pro. But a funny thing happened on her way to the barre: She began performing in roles in school plays that weren't all musicals. And she found she liked acting.

She also learned a tough lesson. "It was always the same kids getting picked for roles, getting accolades, kudos. They're the 4.0 students, popular, smart, the stars. But a lot of kids don't get noticed at all." She was one of those. "It seems like a logical progression

117

from dance, but I was never the leader, the thespian, the one picked to be in the lead role. I was always in the chorus, involved somehow, but not the star."

She didn't exactly rule the social scene in either school. "I had a pretty hard time in high school," she admitted to a journalist. "I was picked on because my hair was too permed."

She also resented having to wear a uniform for ballet, as well as the ban on jewelry. "I thought it was stupid stuff schools do just to exercise authority. Just because I'm not wearing the right color leotard doesn't make me any less serious."

Academics were not where she excelled. She didn't actually flunk out, but calls herself the kind of kid who was hard to reach. There was one plus, however, to her high-school years: She finally grew into her name. "I ended up liking it, and I've gone by nothing else ever since."

## "Are You an Actress?"

Dancing and being in school productions did not allow her to "pass go" straight into an acting career. Her path to Sunnydale High was totally circuitous. After her high-school graduation, she did a bunch of things unrelated to acting or dancing. She toured Europe extensively, then returned to San Diego and took jobs in real estate, in a video store, and as an aerobics instructor. Then, she auditioned for and won a gig as a San Diego Chargers cheerleader.

After that, she moved to Los Angeles to become . . . a teacher. While going to school to get her degree, she waitressed in a restaurant — where she was constantly asked if she was an actress. Finally, she just decided to try her luck in showbiz. She got an agent and almost immediately booked a commercial. It was for Secret Ultra Dry deodorant — and it ran for two years.

Encouraged, Charisma joined Playhouse West and finally studied acting. She performed in many stage productions there, including the musical *No, No, Nanette.* All the time, she paid the rent by doing other commercials; she has over twenty to her credit. "Being on commercials is funny," she commented to *Jump* magazine. "No one ever recognizes you [from them]. They just come up and say, 'Did I go to school with you?' Or, 'Where do I know you from?'"

Her first movie role was in a grade-B little-seen flick called *Timemaster*. And then, she hit the beach — a guest gig on *Baywatch* led to *Malibu Shores*, a 1996 NBC midseason series. The show, which ended up being short-lived, was memorable for a few reasons. It was produced by *90210/Melrose Place* king, Aaron Spelling. It costarred Tori's brother, Randy Spelling, and also — notably — Keri Russell, now Charisma's WB mate in the new show *Felicity*.

On *Malibu Shores,* Charisma played Ashley, the "bad, snobby girl," as she once described the character, who makes life miserable for the nice-girl leads. Even she admits it wasn't a huge stretch from that role to *Buffy's* Cordelia.

## "As Long as We're Strong and Healthy, We Should Be Proud of Who We Are"

Not that she actually auditioned for that role at first. Charisma went to the *Buffy* tryouts wearing overalls and flip-flops — she thought she was testing for the lead role. "But they decided I would make a much better Cordelia," she says. And so she did.

"I'm much friendlier than Cordelia is," Charisma has revealed. "I'm more outgoing, more approachable. I love to dance, run, go

Rollerblading. I've even gone skydiving." Or, as she put it once, "As opposed to some of the prissy characters I've played, who perspire — in real life, I sweat!"

Even though Cordelia has grown and changed lots, Charisma believes there's still much more to her TV persona than meets the eye. The actress even devised a little back story for the character. "In one episode, Cordelia mentioned her mom being sick, so I decided that maybe Cordelia has been ignored at home, and so all the sarcastic comments she makes at school are just a way to wield some power, and to survive. She's a survivor.

"She's definitely the counterpoint to Buffy and her friends," Charisma continues. "Even though she's one of them now, she retains her edge; she's still the one making the 'smart' comments."

When quizzed about her TV name, Charisma explains that Cordelia has nothing to do with the character from the famous Shakespearean play *King Lear*. Instead, it was inspired by a friend of Joss Whedon's wife who was a snob in school. "I didn't like it," the actress reveals, "but [it] grew on me like my own name did."

There are some places where the fictional Cordelia and the real-life Charisma connect. "When I was in high school, if I saw [a boy] I liked, I'd go after him. I was never quite as 'out there' as Cordelia. I had more subtlety, but like her, I'm a person who goes after anything I want or need."

Plus, there's this connection: "Cordelia likes clothes, I like clothes. She likes boys, I like boys." Of course, not exactly the same kind of clothes — or boys. The former, in fact, has been a huge issue for Charisma, especially in the show's first season.

Back then, it seemed as if Cordelia's skirts were shorter than those any of the other female cast members had to wear. Granted, the micro-minis weren't out of character for show-off Cordelia — but they were massively uncomfortable for the actress, who once gasped to a reporter, "I would never wear dresses that short — oh, God, no — no way. I like to dress outrageously, but not in skirts that short. And then there was the episode where I wore the tightest pants ever. I was miserable."

The reason? She explained, "Everybody has their thing — one aspect of their body that they don't really care for. Mine's my bubble butt. I'm asked to wear things I don't like or feel comfortable wearing, but I can't just go and say to the wardrobe person, 'No, I'm not wearing this.'"

She did, however, have a little talk with the wardrobe department. The upshot was not that Cordelia's clothes got lengthened so much but that Charisma ended up with a different point of view. As she explained, "The wardrobe person is Scandinavian and she couldn't understand my reluctance to wear something that accentuates a body part I didn't feel good about. She explained that females come in all shapes and sizes, and we shouldn't feel self-conscious about our bodies. As long as we're strong and healthy, we should just be proud of who we are. And I realized that if I could, by my celebrity, convey that to girls out there, that would be a good thing. So I stopped worrying about what Cordy was wearing."

But not about who Cordy was dating. In some ways, she even overidentifies with her TV alter ego. "I get jealous for her," Charisma revealed. "Especially in that episode where Xander and Buffy were dancing. I was like, 'Wait, aren't we supposed to be going out?'"

## "I've Had a Broken Heart"

Naturally, one of the questions she gets asked most often is about her real-life relationship with Nicholas Brendon, Xander. "I love Nicky," she told *YM*. "He's my buddy." But they're not an off-screen couple.

Charisma has had boyfriends throughout her school years; however, the relationships didn't always work out. In fact, being pretty, smart, sweet, confident, and successful never shielded her from heartbreak — like everyone else, Charisma's done time in the "I've Been Dumped" club. She openly revealed in an interview, "I've dated the cool type. It was always short-lived, and I always wound up with a broken heart. I've had a broken heart many times, starting at age eleven — the first time a boy dumped me for another girl."

Just before she started *Malibu Shores,* she endured yet another breakup. "The breakup had nothing to do with showbiz. And I really didn't see it coming," she confessed to reporters.

Right now, she's single and open to meeting someone special. "At one point, I said I wouldn't date an actor, but then someone pointed out to me that an actor has to know himself and plunge into the depths of his soul

124

to know himself better. Wouldn't you want to be with someone like that?"

## Looking Ahead

Perhaps the biggest news for Charisma's fans is that she's been signed to costar on David's upcoming *Angel* show. She'll still be Cordelia, and like Angel she'll continue to pop up on *Buffy* as well.

Charisma would like to nab a big-screen role one day, but she's in no particular rush. "I want longevity. I want to last and do the best possible job I can," is her career goal.

The biggest rush, in fact, is the one she gets from being on *Buffy*. She describes the feeling of acting in it and then seeing the finished product on TV. "It's like, WOW, WOW, WOW! It's like being in the forest among the trees — you can't see the whole picture until you're outside of it. Every episode is like a minimovie. I'm pretty proud of it."

# 11

# Seth Green as Oz

*"I Don't Take Myself Seriously,
but I Take What I Do Seriously"*

**M**ust be something in the Buff-ified air:
Count Seth Green as the *third* part-
time recurring character to be promoted to
full-fledged regular. Good news for him, boda-
cious bulletin for Seth's millions of fans. He
plays high-school student by day, musician by
night Oz — not exactly as in, the "great and
powerful," but certainly as in, the hip, happy,
and hirsute!

Hip because after all, he's a boy in the
band; happy comes courtesy of Willow, Oz's
one-time crush object and current full-time
girlfriend. As for the hirsute part . . . well,
this *is Buffy the Vampire Slayer.* Adding another totally normal person to the cast wasn't

an option. True, a couple of days a month Oz isn't quite himself: He gets the hair thing going on big time and turns into a creature-of-the-night werewolf. Whatever. Willow loves her bass-playing boyfriend unconditionally. And so do we.

## "I Couldn't Have a Normal High-School Experience. . . . "

Must be an East Coast thing: Sarah's from New York; Alyson's an Atlantan. Count Seth Green as the *fourth Buffy* star to hail from "back east," and the *second* (after David) to call the City of Brotherly Love — Philadelphia — home. The carrot-topped youngest child of Herb and Barbara Gesshel-Green grew up in West Philadelphia, a scene stealer from the start. Outgoing, dramatic, funny, precocious, and creative, Seth was pretty much to showbiz born. He wanted to be on TV or in the movies. That is, he *really* wanted it. "I just pushed and pushed," he admitted online. "Sometimes you just know what you want to do."

Hurdle alert: Dad was a math teacher, Mom an artist, and Philadelphia wasn't exactly Hollywood. No biggie. Seth, age six, with help from Mom and his godfather's

127

brother — a casting director — hooked up with a local talent manager. She promptly sent him to nearby (well, okay, three hours away) New York City to start auditioning for kiddie roles.

Success came swiftly.

As in, immediately. Seth nailed his first showbiz gig, an RCA Records promotion for John Denver, the day after he signed with his manager.

As in, fast and furiously. The cute little kid with uncanny performing abilities soon booked commercials for such biggies as Burger King, Kodak, and Rally's fast food. He also appeared in public service ads — he did a bit in a gas mask — and then, kerplunk, he landed on the big screen. Not just any big screen. At age eight, Seth debuted in the movie *Hotel New Hampshire*. It starred Rob Lowe, Jodie Foster, and Natassia Kinski. At age twelve, he took a call from Woody Allen, auditioned for the legendary writer/director/actor, and landed his first movie lead in *Radio Days*.

As in, too soon? Looking back, Seth thinks maybe yes. His official bio admits he was cocky, especially when he got to be a guest on

*The Tonight Show With Johnny Carson,* trading quips with the king of late night TV. Did he get bratty? He sort of cops to it. "You get wrapped up in the money and having people tell you how great you are. You forget that you are pretending."

Unsurprisingly, all that nonstop fame and acclaim affected his real life. While commuting back and forth to New York for auditions, Los Angeles for roles, and all over the globe for location shoots, Seth remained enrolled in public school in Philadelphia. Where he encountered lots of problems. "I couldn't have a normal high-school experience because I was acting and had to leave in the middle of the day and take all my homework with me and take a train to New York and go on auditions," he told *USA Today.* He also sometimes had grade trouble — but after a GPA meltdown, he got his priorities straight and hit the books. In the end? Seth graduated high school — with honors.

He might have followed his peers and gone on to college, but by that time, Seth was deeply immersed in the biz — and, to quasi-paraphrase one of his latest movies, "couldn't hardly wait" to do it full-time.

## It's Seth's World — We Just Live in It

Count Seth Green as the . . . well, first, actually . . . *Buffy* star to make his mark in the movies. As opposed to his cast mates, who are doing the small-to-big-screen boogie, Seth started in film and is only now doing regular TV.

After his childhood roles in *Hotel New Hampshire* and *Radio Days*, Seth rocked the big screen, big time. In *Big Business*, he played Bette Midler's issue-plagued son. Throughout his teen years, he appeared in *Can't Buy Me Love*, *Pump Up the Volume*, *Ticks*, and *Airborne*. And another, *My Stepmother Is an Alien*, where he first met his *Buffy* love, Alyson Hannigan.

Being *Buffy*'s Oz is his biggest TV break, but it's far from Seth's first time on TV. After the miniseries *Stephen King's It*, he did a not-long-for-this-world *Facts of Life* spin-off series, then ABC's short-lived *Good and Evil*, CBS's aptly named *Temporarily Yours*, and first crossed professional paths briefly with Jennifer Love Hewitt in *The Byrds of Paradise* (he played her brother). A slew of guest-star gigs followed, including bits on *The X-Files*, *Mad About You*, and *The Drew Carey Show*.

Perhaps Seth's most widely seen performance, pre-*Buffy*, was in the quirky hit movie *Austin Powers: International Man of Mystery*. He played Scott Evil, Dr. Evil's estranged son. Meeting Mike Myers, who starred as the title character *and* Dr. Evil, was a kick. "He's a classy guy," said Seth, who just agreed to reprise his role in the sequel. On the heels of *Austin Powers,* he was asked to do a voice-over as the cat in the "new" *Dr. Dolittle.*

He reteamed with his TV sis, Jennifer Love Hewitt, in the 1998 summertime teen comedy *Can't Hardly Wait,* a flick he felt almost nostalgic about. "When I was growing up there were all these John Hughes movies, all these teen-oriented movies," he mentioned in an interview. "I think kids [now] are just looking for something they can relate to. They want to see something fun and entertaining." He played wanna-be homeboy Kenny Fisher totally convincingly. Talking the hip-hop talk was easy, as he explained to *USA Today.* "My friends and I talk like that all the time. I listened to a lot of *Yo! MTV Raps.* Watch anything with Puffy Combs, you're on it."

Behind the scenes was as much fun as

what the cameras caught. "Everywhere on that set," Seth remembers, "I loved going to work. Everybody on the movie was awesome. We were never not having a good time."

It was while camping it up in *Can't Hardly Wait* that *Buffy the Vampire Slayer* popped up on his radar screen.

## Oz, the Unflappable

When Seth met with *Buffy* creator Joss Whedon to test for the role of Oz, he was given a tip about the character. "Joss said, 'Oz would have the same reaction to spray cheese as to true love. He's unflappable.'" Seth was into it. "I love being the guitar player on TV; I'm living out my rock 'n' roll fantasy."

It was only supposed to be four episodes. But Willow and — more important — viewers were all over Oz. So they made it five episodes. Then eight. Season two ended with the signing of Seth to all twenty-six this year. "The show is so fun and quirky but there's a lot of heart to it, that's what's so appealing. It's smart, scary, and fun," raves Seth. "They take their monsters seriously without the show taking itself too seriously."

## What He's Really, Really Like

It seems like Seth has little time for an actual life, since his pretend one is so hectic. He does, however, manage to squeeze in a few off-camera activities. "I read a ton of magazines," he admitted. "I play pool; I love to see any movie that's out, good or bad." In fact, he actually thinks the one bad thing about *making* films is less time for *watching* them. Which all sounds fairly Oz-esque.

One big difference between reel life and real life is that Seth doesn't have a girlfriend right now — he's not dating Alyson Hannigan. He does, however, hang out with a bunch of actor friends. But he's not a name-dropper — nor has hanging with the hip Hollywood crowd made him forget the people who are really important. Even three thousand miles from where he grew up, Seth remains close to his family. "My mom is really cool, and super independent. My parents are my role models."

More Seth personality profile: He's modest. "I've been incredibly fortunate. I've worked with the best people . . . who make me look better than I am." And he totally appreciates the people who appreciate him. "I'm thrilled by my fans," he asserts.

## Idle Hands? Well, Yes.

Just because he has the *Buffy* deal doesn't mean the big screen will be Seth-challenged. Not even close. He's got a small role in a big movie called *Enemy of the State,* with Will Smith. "I'm the surveillance guy who's had too much caffeine and lives in the van."

And then there's a big role in a small independent film called *Stonebrook.* "I play Cornelius Webber, a guy who helps his college roommate pay tuition through a series of staged sting operations. I get to play a lot of different characters in each con. As usual, all hell breaks loose and their world comes crashing down."

Which leads to something Seth could clearly never relate to: *Idle Hands.* That's the name of his newest flick, described as a teen slacker/slasher film. It stars Devon Sawa (*Casper, Wild America*) as Anton, a seventeen-year-old slacker who suddenly discovers that one of his hands is . . . possessed by the devil. And the hand, of its own free will, has forced him to kill his parents and his best friends. But the friends come back as zombies. Mick as a headless zombie, that would be Seth, who admits, "This is unlike anything people have ever seen before, because you won't know who to root for."

## Future Drama

So . . . what's next for the hardest-working werewolf on TV? Because he's been in the business so long, Seth has read a ton of scripts. He admits to being fully boggled by "the amount of awful scripts that get produced, and the most incredible stories that never get made." He dreams of becoming a producer one day, so the good stories get a chance to be told cinematically. While he's fantasizing, Seth dreams of creating roles for all his actor buds. "I'd like to get all my friends together and make a movie once a year," he wrote.

Beyond that, he has another attainable goal. "I always want to work hard, to appreciate [the roles] I am getting and to always be working. I don't take myself seriously, but I take what I do seriously. I'm just so excited to have a job that I do what I can to make it fun for the cast, the crew, and anyone else willing to watch." Which pretty much covers . . . everyone.

# 12

# Camp *Buffy*: A Day Behind the Scenes

So you want to be a vampire slayer? Or at least the friend of one? Check out the behind-the-scenes vibe, but watch your neck if you don't want to be disillusioned — here come the reality bites.

## Being There

The fictional Sunnydale is actually two real-life places, neither of which has any reason to believe there's a Hellmouth underneath — so far, anyway.

Torrence High School, in a near-the-airport L.A. suburb, plays the part of Sunnydale High. If it looks familiar, that's because the *90210* kids "went" there, too. The *Buffy* cast invades after hours or on school holidays. Since it's an outdoor set at a public school that's the place fans often come to watch the show being filmed, and sometimes get up close with a cast member. Although everyone is flattered by the attention, Alyson and Charisma are notable for going out of their way to be friendly to fans.

A decidedly unglam Santa Monica warehouse "plays" the other part of Sunnydale. Indoor scenes such as Giles's library, the Bronze, the vampires' lair, and the Buffster's bedroom, are shot there. Santa Monica is just outside L.A. city limits, but far enough from the studio back lot, where most TV shows are filmed. And that makes all the difference.

"There's not a lot of ego running around, like who has the bigger trailer, stuff like that," tipped David Boreanaz in *Seventeen* magazine. "If we were in a big studio lot, it would really break up the show. With the amount of time spent applying makeup and setting up special effects, it's good that we have a camp like this. It's our own little home."

A visit to either *Buffy* location finds mostly same-size trailers parked outside. Those are the dressing rooms and, okay, there are *some* differences. You can figure out which one is

Sarah's because of the aroma of vanilla incense wafting from it — and it is slightly bigger than the others. Nicky's is the one from which the loud music is usually blasting.

Each cast member has a director's chair with his or her name stitched onto the back. Sarah's white Maltese puppy, Thor, often sits in hers.

## The Real Deal on the Special Effects

According to Alyson, just driving onto either set is awesome. "When you park your car, you see 'demons' hanging out in the parking lot!" Of course, becoming demons — through the magic of makeup and special effects — isn't always so much fun. The actors who play the vampires — including David — have to report to the set earlier than the others, in order to get their makeup done. The vamp faces are actually masks that fit from the forehead to the bridge of the nose. The actors usually lie down when the mask is attached — they "rise" looking very different! "It takes about an hour and twenty minutes to get the mask on," David says. "Faster to get it off, because it's a prosthetic. It's like Robin's mask in *Batman*. They paint it over a prosthetic, and use makeup to blend it in. It's

138

the blending that takes the most time. Then, you put in the contact lenses and the teeth and you're ready to rock 'n' roll."

Becoming a werewolf takes more time — just ask Seth Green, *Buffy*'s resident teen howler. "It takes a lot of time and it's really difficult to stand still. It starts at eleven-thirty and goes until four-thirty. They have to hand lay all of the hair on me but the makeup artists are so great, so sweet and considerate. They make it as painless as possible, and the end result is worth the effort."

The effort spent on making the special effects ultracool paid off with 1998 Emmy nominations for best hair and makeup (as well as one for music). Maybe that's why Alyson admits, "There really isn't anything scary. Once you see the people behind the set, the monsters are a lot less scary."

## The Big Ouch

If the monsters aren't real, the injuries inflicted sometimes are. Sarah has a well-earned rep for the black and blue — due, no doubt, to her well-earned rep for bravery, above and beyond her call of duty. Of course she has a stunt double, and naturally the

fight scenes are professionally choreo-
graphed, but just the same, Sarah sometimes
volunteers for combat duty. "Crash through a
window? Jump off a balcony? I'll say, 'I can do
that,' and a lot of times they let me."

And a lot of times, she's got the scars to
show for it — mostly physical, but sometimes
emotional. David recalled the season-ending
fight scene between Angel and Buffy where
she sends him to some section of the great beyond. "We got into a groove, we focused and
let it fly. When it was over, we didn't want it
to end." Sarah added, "That sword scene was
incredible. I was crying afterwards."

Sarah's not the only one prone to injuries.
Nicky once hit his head after falling off a wall
because, according to Alyson, his "male-ego
pride" got in the way of the pad he should
have allowed to be put down to cushion the
blow.

## "If Anyone Could Get Milk to Come Through My Nose, It Would Be Nicky"

Need proof that the slayer and the slayer-
ettes bond much when the cameras aren't
rolling? Here's what they've said.

In an on-line interview, Alyson asserted,
"The whole cast is like a family. Everyone is

wonderful; we really have the best time. Our job is the best job."

Charisma added, "Everybody's so awesome. Nicky keeps people in stitches. He's shy, but funny. The persona he exudes is so different from who he really is. You can have a heart-to-heart with him, but he's also a prankster. He's like two people."

Charisma's in awe of her female costars. "Sarah's so devoted to her craft — sometimes I wonder how she does it. And Ally is so fun, the funniest girl I know. She's so great, earthy and funny and bright."

Nicky told *Teenbeat* magazine, "It's like a family. We all get stressed out on the set sometimes, but who doesn't?"

Practical jokes, they've learned, are major stress busters. Nicky recalls, "During the hyena episode from the first season, I got pantsed [pants pulled down] by Alyson — there were about forty extras around."

Alyson places blame elsewhere. "It was Sarah's idea! But she chickened out and I did it by myself. During the first season, we were doing a scene at the gym. Nicky was wearing sweatpants — I accidentally took down his boxers at the same time. I felt really bad, and I'll never live it down!"

Although Nicky warns, "I will pay her back," he actually got to Anthony Stewart Head (Giles) first. On the last shot of his last day, Nicky threw a whipped cream pie in his face. Icing: The actor had an audition right after.

Alyson, however, is fully forewarned. "If anyone could get milk to come through my nose, it would be Nicky."

The joking around even extends to the romantic scenes. "Before doing kissing scenes," David confesses, "Sarah and I try to gross each other out by eating things like Goldfish crackers, Doritos, and tuna fish. We know it's disgusting, but we love it."

And to the tragic scenes. "It's hard not for us to giggle," Alyson admitted. "Sarah and I are the worst! We have to start thinking about dead animals to stop laughing! It's so much fun, though."

## One Huge Cuddlefest

Whether they're playing practical jokes or grossing one another out, the undercurrent vibe is one of mutual respect and support. The stars often mill around the soundstages, trading one-ups, comparing notes, and riffing about the latest movie, concert, or restaurant

142

someone's been to lately. Lots of hugs and back rubs are given and gratefully received. And because we're in the reality zone here — the occasional rubbing one another the wrong way happens, too. Especially during those temper-fraying fifteen-hour workdays.

Sarah told *Seventeen* magazine, "No one gets along 24/7. When I was having a bad day, everyone stayed away from me. I went to my trailer and watched soap operas and then I felt better."

But what about the green monster? Is there ever any jealousy? Doesn't seem to be. When the show got successful, Charisma told *TV Guide,* "Sarah got a bigger trailer, but nobody got more money."

## Hanging Together Off the Set

Proof positive that the *Buffy* cast really are friends: These guys hang together even when they don't have to.

Nicky said, "We call each other when we're not working, and we hang out. We go out to dinner for each other's birthdays. We talk to each other constantly, when we're down or something's bothering us."

Getting together for b-days is becoming a *Buffy* tradition. *TV Guide* reported on the twenty-fourth birthday celebration the cast attended for Alyson Hannigan. It was held in a huge Hollywood loft, decorated in vampire chic. Three rock bands played. Sarah arrived fashionably late with a posse of gal pals.

Show nights are becoming another tradition as cast members gather to watch the show together. Not that they discuss amongst themselves when it's over. "We don't talk about acting when we're together, just hang out," Sarah said, adding that when it's just her, Ally, and Charisma, they "get silly, get girly."

## Bonding Buds, Guys: Nicky and David

Nicky says, "David Boreanaz is actually one of my best friends. It started in the first season, when we went to the park, walked his dog, talked about stuff. There was an instant connection." David agrees, "We talk all the time, between scenes mostly, and we hang out together afterwards."

## Bonding Buds, Girls: Sarah and Alyson

A year ago, Ally (as her buds call her) ended up in the hospital for a tonsillectomy. She woke up from surgery to find Sarah at her bedside, bearing yogurt and a get well

144

gift — a Beanie Baby. That was sweet, but exchanging gag gifts is what the two have become known for. "We have ongoing jokes," Alyson revealed. "Sarah and I are always buying each other silly presents. Just before Christmas, she gave me this singing Christmas tree. And I'm convinced it's Harry Connick's voice on it! It's really loud and it's scared me a few times. She put it on my trailer and it scared me to death!"

Alyson gave Sarah a rather bizarre doll that can blow bubbles — from a place *Ace Ventura* fans would find hysterical. Sarah noted, "My gifts are funny; hers are disgusting!"

The girls keep in touch wherever they are. When Sarah went to New York to host *Saturday Night Live*, she held up a sign saying she missed Alyson!

## Bonding Buds, Four-Footed Kind

Something else that keeps the cast connected: They're all (except Seth, so far) dog owners.

# 13

# Quick Bites
# on the Slayer Team

## *Suddenly Sarah*

**Full Name:** Sarah Michelle Gellar
**Nickname:** Spence (originated during her
gig on TV's *Spencer: For Hire*)
**Birthday:** April 14, 1977
**Zodiac Sign:** Aries. She believes she's a typ-
ical Aries.
**Height:** 5'3"
**Hair:** It's naturally dark. She blonds it for
*Buffy*.
**Eye Color:** Green
**Family:** Mom is Rosellen; Dad is Steven; no
sisters or brothers; stepdad

**Born In:** New York City
**Grew Up In:** New York City
**Education:** Graduate of Professional Children's School
**Now Lives In:** The Hollywood Hills section of Los Angeles

**Roll the Credits**
**Stage:** *The Widow Claire, Jake's Women*
**TV Guest Spots:** *Spencer: For Hire, Guiding Light, Girl Talk*
**TV Voice-overs:** *King of the Hill*, as Bobby's girlfriend
**TV Movie:** *A Woman Named Jackie, Invasion of Privacy*
**TV Series:** *All My Children, Swan's Crossing, Buffy the Vampire Slayer*
**Commercials:** *Burger King*
**Movies:** *I Know What You Did Last Summer, Scream 2, Cruel Inventions, Vanilla Fog*
**Wish Role:** A cameo on *Dawson's Creek*

**Favorites**
**Movies:** *Heathers, Grosse Point Blank*
**Actors:** John Cusack, Daniel Day Lewis, Stockard Channing, Tom Cruise, and Eric Stoltz "because he's the cutest"

**Music:** Billy Joel, Phil Collins

**TV:** *Seinfeld* and *Murphy Brown*

**Color:** Red

**Food:** Although she's careful to cut the sugar, Sarah lists soup, pasta, and Chinese as her fave cuisine.

**Drink:** Water, iced tea, Starbucks decaf coffee

**Book:** Dr. Seuss's *There's a Wocket in My Pocket,* because of the line, "There's a gellar in the cellar." Also, *Gone With the Wind.*

**Sports Team:** New York Giants

**Sports:** Tae kwon do, hiking, Rollerblading, ice skating, waterskiing

**Fragrance:** Amarige by Givenchy, Chanel's Allure

**Potions:** Anything vanilla. "I love any kind of vanilla body lotion. I always have candles in my trailer and for my bath."

**Indulgence:** Manicures and pedicures

**Car:** A red truck

**Designer:** Shelli Segal (Laundry)

**Shoes:** Steve Madden

**Fashion Don'ts:** "Basically, the only things I don't like are anything tight and short, or bright pastel colors. Shoulder pads are coming back and I hate them! I'm a tiny person so if I have shoulder pads on, you know it."

**Favorite Holiday:** Halloween

**Least Favorite Holiday:** Valentine's Day. "It's a miserable holiday," she told *Seventeen* magazine. "If you're in a relationship, then this is the one day you're supposed to say I love you and send gifts to ensure it means more than the other 364 days of the year. And if you're single, you feel miserable. In school, I always got roses, but gave them to someone who didn't get any."

**Most Outrageous Thing She's Ever Done:** Cliff diving

**Pets:** A cat and Thor, her Maltese, a white fluff ball

**Pet Peeve:** Interviews

**For Fun:** "Fun? Who has time for fun?" is her joke, but when not working, she figure skates, Rollerblades, power naps — and power shops.

**Most Bizarre Quote:** "My eyebrows are the most unruly things in America."

**Philosophy of Life:** "If you want it, go and get it, because you only have one life to live."

**Salary:** $30,000 per episode — which sounds like a lot, but not when you compare it to the bucks other stars of their own shows are making. Besides, *Entertainment Weekly* says she's worth "twice that."

**Vampires, Yes or No:** That would be a negative.

## Fame, Acclaim, and Awards
**Cover Girl:** Sarah has been a cover girl on several high profile publications, including *Rolling Stone, TV Guide, YM,* and *Seventeen.*
**Hostess with the Mostest:** She hosted on *Saturday Night Live.*
**Awards, Won:** Daytime Emmy for "Outstanding Younger Actress" for *All My Children* in 1995.
**Awards, Nominated:** Blockbuster for "Best Supporting Actress, Horror Movie" for *I Know What You Did Last Summer.*

## *Nick's Nook*

**Full Name:** Nicholas Brendon is actually his first and middle name: Nick prefers keeping his real last name private.
**Nickname:** Nicky
**Birthday:** April 12, 1971
**Zodiac Sign:** Aries
**Height:** 5'11"
**Hair:** Brown
**Eye Color:** Hazel

**Born In:** Grenada Hills, California

**Grew Up In:** Grenada Hills, California

**Family:** Mom and Dad are Kathy and Bob. They divorced when Nicky was eighteen. He has two younger teenage bros, Christian and Kyle, who aren't in showbiz. "They're doing the school thing," Nick says. His identical twin brother is Kelly.

**Switcheroo:** "Once, Kelly and I tried to fool everyone, but we got caught. In sixth grade, we had two sets of twins, and they put us in different classes — we decided to switch classes. The other twins got caught and gave us up."

**Education:** After graduating high school, Nicky logged one year at L.A.'s College of the Canyon before leaving to pursue acting full-time.


**Favorites**

**Actors:** Jack Lemmon, Jim Carrey, Rosie O'Donnell, Johnny Depp

**Movie:** *Some Like It Hot*

**TV:** *The Simpsons, Seinfeld* reruns, *The X-Files*

**Music:** Frank Sinatra, Louis Armstrong, Beck, Cake, Nerf Herder

**Song:** "Sorry," by Nerf Herder

**Does He Sing?** "I sing for my loved ones. I sing in the shower or in the car. Maybe if I weren't acting, I would try to sing. But the public is lucky that I am acting — my singing wouldn't go over too well."

**Food:** Pasta, sushi, and Carnation instant chocolate drink for breakfast

**Color:** Blue

**Book:** *The Giving Tree*

**Car:** Range Rover

**Pet:** Zoey, a once homeless mixed-breed stray dog he took in

**Pet Peeve:** People who drive Humvees. According to Nick, the statement they're making is, "'I have money and I'm going to show it off.' It's ridiculous. They're so large you can't get around them."

**Irrational Fear:** Heights

**On Acting:** "It's like being a kid and playing with Matchbox cars in the dirt again. It's called acting 'cause you make-believe, you pretend."

**Goal:** "To take care of all my friends and family, to stay a nice person."

**First Kiss:** "It was in eighth grade. It sucked because we had friends spying on us. I was embarrassed when we got caught, so I had to break up with her," Nick told *Teen* magazine.

**Talking the Talk:** Occasionally, traces of his old stutter emerge.

**Favorite Phrase:** "Yeah, yeah"

**Vampires, Yes or No:** "I'm into sci-fi to the extent that I like to consider the possibility, what if that stuff was out there? But vampires? Nah."

### Alyson's Angle

**Full Name:** Alyson Hannigan
**Nickname:** Ally
**Birthday:** March 24, 1974
**Zodiac Sign:** Aries
**Born In:** Washington, D.C.
**Grew Up In:** Atlanta, Georgia, and Los Angeles, California
**Now Lives In:** Los Angeles

**Roll the Credits**
**TV Guest Spots:** *Picket Fences, Roseanne, Touched by an Angel*
**TV Movies:** *For My Daughter's Honor, The Stranger Beside Me, Switched at Birth*
**Movies:** *My Stepmother Is an Alien*

**TV Series:** *Almost Home* (the renamed *Torkelsons*), *Free Spirit, Buffy the Vampire Slayer*

**Favorites**

**Actors:** Jodie Foster. Alyson respects her for taking the time to go to college and then come back to her career. Also, Steve Buscemi because "he's so offbeat, such a weirdo, I love him."

**Movie:** *Toy Story*—"I'm obsessed with it."

**TV:** *The X-Files* and *The Simpsons*

**Music:** Cake

**Song:** "I Will Survive"

**Cookies:** Animal crackers

**Style:** Fuzzy sweaters

**Collects:** Beanie Babies

**Computer Literate?:** "I go to the *Buffy* Web site a lot. I am on AOL." That's pretty much the extent of her cyberexperience.

**What She Can't Do:** "I am so not a writer. I can't express myself through writing."

**Secret Ambition:** "To be a cartoon. I just think I would be a good cartoon. I would want to be one of those alien guys that gets to feed the dog."

**Vampires, Yes or No:** Not sure. "I think it's interesting. I've always been intrigued by vampires, anything that's different from everyday normal blasé people. You know, they might exist. They might."

## *David's Deal*

**Full Name:** David Boreanaz Jr.

**You Pronounce It:** Bore-ee-*an*-az. "Like the star [system] Aurora Borealis," he tips.

**Heritage:** Czech (from his dad) and Italian (on his mom's side)

**Birthday:** May 16, 1971

**Zodiac Sign:** Taurus

**Born In:** Buffalo, New York

**Grew Up In:** Philadelphia

**Now Lives In:** The Hollywood Hills

**Height:** 6'1"

**Hair:** Light brown

**Eye Color:** Deep brown

**Family:** Wife, Mom, Dad, two older sisters, two brothers-in-law, several nieces and nephews.

**An "Awww" Moment**: "My parents are very proud. That's the best reward, having my parents see me do this. God bless parents — where would we be without them?"

**Kid Stuff:** "When I was a kid, I got caught playing with Roman candles in cemeteries all the time. Now I really love old cemeteries

155

with those ancient gravestones. They're so spooky."

**First Ambition:** To be a professional football player

**Pets:** Bertha Blue, a four-year-old mixed breed, plus a small Chinese crested powder puff puppy that "could be a circus dog." He loves horses as well and would love to own one eventually.

## Roll the Credits

**Stage Roles:** *Hatful of Rain, Italian-American Reconciliation, Fool for Love, Cowboy Mouth.* The last, a Sam Shepard play, performed in Los Angeles, was his favorite.

**Film Roles:** *Aspen Extreme, Best of the Best 2; Eyes of the World*

**TV Roles:** *Married . . . With Children, Men Don't Lie*

## Favorites

**Actors:** Gary Oldman, Leonardo DiCaprio, Uma Thurman, Gwyneth Paltrow

**Music:** Jazz, blues, and old-time rock 'n' roll

**Least Favorite Music:** Electronica, or "house music"

**Groups:** Grateful Dead, Rolling Stones

**Instrument He Plays:** Harmonica

156

**Food:** Philadelphia cheese steak. "It's the only place on the planet that can get it right."
**Place to Chill:** The lounge at L.A.'s Chateau Marmont hotel because "it's not crowded and you [can] really talk."
**Place to Vacation:** Tahiti
**Time of Day:** Sunset. "There's this glow in the sky; those hours are magical."
**Sports:** Bowling, golf, tennis, skiing, hockey, basketball, boxing
**Word:** "Trippy" — David uses it a lot.
**He Describes Himself:** "I know my heart, and it bleeds for passion. I'm also a rebel; I love to run wild."
**Marital Status:** He's married to his long-time love, Ingrid, a social worker.
**Vampires, Yes or No:** "I've watched all the movies. *Nosferatu* was a really cool film, and I've read all the Anne Rice novels and Lestat is my favorite character — but no, I don't [believe]."

## *Charisma's Corner*

**Full Name:** Charisma Lee Carpenter
**Birthday:** July 23, 1970
**Zodiac Sign:** Leo
**Born In:** Las Vegas, Nevada

**Grew Up In:** San Diego, California

**Family:** Her dad, Don, lives in Chicago; Chris, her mom, lives in Florida. She has two older brothers, Michael Troy and John Kenneth, and several stepsibs since her dad's remarriage.

**Height:** 5'6"

**Hair:** Brown

**Eye Color:** Hazel

**Education:** She graduated high school, but did not go on to college. Still, she feels she's getting a virtual education through her best friend, a UCLA undergrad. "She's an American literature major, so she's giving me reading lists."

**First Ambition:** To be a dancer

**Roll the Credits**

**Commercials:** Secret Ultra Dry

**TV Guest Roles:** *Baywatch*

**TV Series:** *Malibu Shores, Buffy the Vampire Slayer*

**Favorites**

**Actors:** Jack Nicholson, Holly Hunter, Anne Heche

**Movie:** *Legends of the Fall*

**TV:** *Party of Five,* "but there's only one show I schedule my life around: *Buffy!*"
**Music:** Jazz. Paula Cole and the Wallflowers, big time. Charisma has a bit of a history with the latter group. Before they hit it big, a friend used to date a band member and she was always being invited to their live gigs. She never went. "Then, I started hearing the music on the radio and loved it. Then, I saw Jakob Dylan's blue eyes on MTV. Then, I started listening to the words — they're so complex! I still haven't figured out what all the songs mean. And you've gotta love a song you can't figure out in four minutes." She wrote them a fan letter, congratulating them on their success.
**Word:** "Rad"
**Sports:** Rollerblading, skydiving, rock climbing, horseback riding
**Book:** *Charm School* by Nelson Deville
**Place:** Delano Hotel in South Beach, Florida
**For Fun:** Cooking and shopping relax her
**Her Type of Boy:** "The kind that have that brooding, smart thing going on."
**Love Quote:** "The smartest thing I ever did for love was to let go when I wasn't really in it."

**Scared By:** Tarantulas give her the "heebie-jeebies."

**Vampires, Yes or No:** "No! God, I hope they're not for real. I'm not into the whole goth scene. I was never into vampires and blood and gore, but the way they're incorporated into the show is cool. I guess the show has exposed me to [something] I might not have gotten to experience otherwise."

## *Seth Stuff*

**Full Name:** Seth Gesshel-Green
**Birthday:** February 8, 1974
**Zodiac Sign:** Aquarius
**Born In:** Philadelphia, Pennsylvania
**Grew Up In:** West Philadelphia, Pennsylvania
**Family:** Herb, a math teacher, is Seth's pop; artist Barbara is his mom. His sister, Kaela, is older.
**Height:** 5'4"
**Hair:** Red
**Eye Color:** Green
**Education:** Seth is a high-school graduate. He also took acting lessons and for many years attended a summer camp that specialized in drama training.

**Roll the Credits**
**Here are some of Seth's film roles:** *Hotel New Hampshire, Radio Days, Big Business, Pump Up the Volume, My Stepmother Is an Alien, Austin Powers: International Man of Mystery*

**Favorites**
**Actors:** Kevin Spacey, Shirley MacLaine, Kevin Bacon. "I'm one degree from Kevin — which is really exciting!"
**Music:** "I like a lot of music, everything from Green Day to Mad Candy, Deadmen Walking, Tom Waits. I like to see bands live."
**Does He Really Play or Sing?** "Sorry to shatter the illusion, but no. I can strum a guitar, but I have a really hard time with the finger placement. I get into the music and I get distracted."
**Movies:** "I love so many movies it's not even funny," he admitted on-line. "My favorites probably are *Midnight Run* and *Raising Arizona.*"
**Vampires, Yes or No:** "I believe in mythology. I believe there's a lot I can't account for. You can't take responsibility for an entire group of people. I was really into mythology, but I kept running into people that were re-

161

ally into Marilyn Manson, saying, 'I drink blood!'" So that would count as a . . . maybe?

## BONUS FACT FILE: ANTHONY STEWART HEAD

**Plays:** Rupert Giles, the librarian/watcher
**His Destiny:** Giles's duty in life is to protect and steer the slayer toward vanquishing vamps and staying alive.
**Full Name:** Anthony Stewart Head
**Nickname:** Call him Tony. Everyone does. It's a better fit than his official stage name — or his uptight character Rupert Giles — would have you believe. Though he is "veddy" British.
**Born In:** Camdentown, England
**Grew Up In:** Hampton, England
**Now Lives In:** Both England and Los Angeles, California
**Education:** London Academy of Music and Dramatic Art

### Roll the Credits
**Stage:** Where he first made his mark. He played Jesus in *Godspell* in London's West End theater district, and then performed in

*The Rocky Horror Picture Show, Julius Caesar, The Heiress, Chess,* and others.

**On Screen, Across the Pond:** BBC Productions, *Enemy at the Door, Love in a Cold Climate*

**On Screen, Here:** He was a regular on the sci-fi series *V.R. 5* and guested on *Highlander* and *NYPD Blue.* Movies he's made include *A Prayer for the Dying.*

**Pre-Buffster He Was Best Known As:** The Taster's Choice dude! Tony was the male part of the love equation between two neighbors who shared a passion . . . for instant coffee. And each other. There were twelve commercials in total.

## What You Really Want to Know:
## The Truth About the Rumors

**Sarah's quitting the show.**
**No.** This rumor was in *TV Guide,* apparently started when someone allegedly overheard Sarah complaining about the disparity between her TV salary and what she could be making in the movies.

It was further fueled in *USA Today* when she complained, "Buffy's been a lot of pressure. I'm in every scene, and there's a lot riding on me. For the films, I was a member of an ensemble, and that was a lot of fun."

Her past history — of seeming to quit *All My Children* right after she won the Emmy Award — hasn't helped quell this rumor, either. But this has: It's been a year since the rumor started, and she's still on the show!

**Sarah's dating David.**

**No.** Though it isn't unheard-of for reel-life hookups to become real life hookups, that was never the case with Sarah and David, who plays Angel. It surely isn't now, since he's a newlywed.

**Buffy tanked in the ratings.**

It used to. When the show first went on the air, it was only a "crit hit" — that is, the critics loved it, but audiences hadn't found it. So out of 107 shows rated, Buffy would come in around 103! However, the second season was the charm. Among girls, especially, the ratings jumped a whopping 217 percent. The WB network is thrilled and has used *Buffy* to anchor its new Tuesday night lineup, which includes, of course, *Dawson's Creek*.

**Sarah smokes.**
Her character did in *I Know What You Did* —
but Sarah off-screen? Uh-uh. No way. Too
health-conscious, and besides, it grosses her
out.

**She's as strong as Buffy is.**
Nooooo. And she doesn't have to slay vampires, either. She is very athletic, though.

**Reaching the Cast**
Snail Mail: c/o *Buffy the Vampire Slayer,* WB-
TV, 4000 Warner Blvd., Burbank, CA 91522.

Cyber Mail: Try AOL's Buffy site, keyword:
Extra